THE MARI
LISA MON

Cara Carvalho and Devin Michaels became best friends one distant summer, until fate and their own inner need for success forced them to separate. Now both are seeking more from their lives. A glib promise on the back of her seventeenth birthday card is enough to bring them together again. Can they have a second chance at happiness?

I enjoyed this novel greatly. The author Lisa Mondello is able to balance the sizzling romance between the couple with more comedic elements into a satisfying whole. She has created a truly modern couple in Cara and Devin. Both are driven by passion for work, but there is more to life than their careers, as they soon discover.

The secondary characters help create a very believable world, and the setting is lush and described so well it made me want to go there immediately for a vacation. Once again, Ms. Mondello has produced a beautifully constructed and compelling romance which readers from 16 to 60 will simply love.

Evelyn Trimborn, author of *Heedless Hearts*

What a lovely romance! I found a real kindred spirit in gutsy Cara, the modern woman trying to have it all. She juggles her family commitments and her hopelessly arrogant boyfriend Roger, all the while knowing that she wants true romance in her life. She gets a second chance at happiness through "the marriage contract" she and Devin made many years before, and they both finally realize that they are made for one another.

Some of the obstacles in their way are very real, if also hilarious at times. Roger is one character you will love to hate, and her grandmother is out of this world, quite literally at times. Ms. Mondello's quality of writing is admirable; she is able to describe elegant settings and events with consummate ease. The romantic summer was never written about so well!

The novel is a moving one which shows that love truly can conquer all. Put this one in your to be read pile or else!

Michaela Brennan, author of *Campaign for Love*

Also by the author

Nothing But Trouble

THE MARRIAGE CONTRACT

Enjoy the laughter!
Lisa Mondello

LISA MONDELLO

DOMHAN BOOKS

ISBN: 1-58345-471-3 paper
1-58345-472-1 disk
1-58345-473-X e book
1-58345-474-8 Millennium
1-58345-475-6 Rocket

Published by Domhan Books

Domhan, pronounced DOW-ann, is the Irish word for universe. Our vision is to bring the reading public all genres of books from new writers all over the world.

9511 Shore Road, Suite 514
Brooklyn New York 11209

Printed and distributed by
Lightning Print/
Ingram Industries
La Vergne, Tennessee 37086

Chapter One

Cara Cavarlho could think of a hundred places she wanted to be right now. This wasn't one of them.

She tugged on the rope dangling above her head. A musty cloud of dust hit her in the face as the stairs leading to the attic of her parents' Westport home dropped down. Gripping the splintered stair rail, she began her ascent into the "black hole", as she had affectionately dubbed the attic in her childhood. She felt a swarm of very mixed emotions. Ever since her parents had decided to sell the family home and move to Florida with the senior league, she had found herself becoming overwhelmed with nostalgia.

Of course, her thirty-fifth birthday being right around the corner didn't help. That her mother kept reminding her of her single, childless status only added to her emotional turmoil.

She yanked on the metal chain dangling above her head and light quickly spilled into the sweltering crawl space.

"It's a furnace up here!" she called down, allowing the cool air from below to bathe her warm face.

Whose idea was it to delve into this black hole on a hot August afternoon? Certainly not mine! she fumed silently.

"I know. We should have done this earlier in the day, before the sun had a chance to heat the attic," she heard her mother, Ruthie, call up from below. "Do you want me to get the fan?"

I want to get out of here and not do this. "No. I can't stay up here long, anyway. I'm already melting."

She carefully crawled along the aged planks, feeling them bend under her weight. Aerobics twice a week and running three miles a day had her wearing the same size she had worn since college, but with each creak of the aged floor boards, she was glad she'd taken pains to keep her figure trim.

She squinted her eyes and tried to focus on the contents of the attic. *Boxes.* There were loads of them scattered helter-skelter around her, tucked into corners and long forgotten. The life she used to lead was lost up here. Why couldn't things ever remain the same...?

"Just start with a few, dear. We can rummage through them down here, and price anything you want to include in the tag sale," Ruthie suggested.

"Sounds like a good idea. I'll come back up tomorrow morning before breakfast to get more. I can barely breathe up here now."

Cara's eyes roamed the piles of memories one last time. After choosing the five boxes closest to the hole and carefully lowering them to her mother, Cara descended into fresh air once again.

She helped her mother drag the boxes down the stairs and out onto the back porch of the beachfront home. Plopping the last one on the wrought iron patio table, she puffed her cheeks and slid the back of her hand across her sweating forehead. *The sooner we get through this the better.*

Ruthie was the first to begin the unveiling, and plunged into a box while Cara poured both of them a tumbler of her mother's homemade lemonade. After a few minutes of digging, Cara found her tension begin to ease. While she'd been dreading the idea of unearthing old memories, she found the task easier once she delved in and became lost in her memories.

The first box was filled with old Christmas ornaments and treasures she and her brother, Manny, had made in school when they'd been kids. A paper doll chain. A old wooden whale Manny had made in woodshop.

The next box had old crochetted blankets and booties from when they had been babies. While Cara fingered the soft yarn of a baby afghan, Ruthie dived into the box filled with old yearbooks and newspaper clippings from Manny's athletic high school days.

"You suppose Manny would want to keep any of these things?" Ruthie asked, picking up a yearbook and fanning the pages open. A candied piece of what looked like edible underwear fell to the floor boards by their feet. Ruthie retrieved the "article" and held it up in the air between her fingers.

Cara laughed, remembering the gag gift Manny had given her years ago. It was harmless, but she knew her mother wouldn't find the truth so humorous.

"Those are mine, Ma. Manny gave them to me before he left for the seminary."

As she expected, Ruthie threw her an appalled look. "How would your brother know about such things? He's a priest, for goodness sake!"

Cara sobered immediately, sucking in her cheeks to keep her laughter at bay. She knew her mother had a hard time remembering Manny as a normal everyday teenager before he'd left for the seminary.

As usual, Cara didn't leave well enough alone. She reached across the table for the naughty underwear. "What size are they, anyway?"

"Never you mind." Ruthie dropped the brittle article of "clothing" in the green rubber garbage can by the table. "If your grandmother saw this, she'd probably take them for herself."

Cara gasped. "She would not!"

"Oh, you'd be surprised. The other day I caught her standing in front of the full-length mirror, trying on one of those tight bustieres Madonna wears all the time."

"You're kidding. You *are* kidding, aren't you?"

Ruthie sighed heavily, a worried looked suddenly etching her face. "I think she has Alzheimer's."

Cara's hand flew to her chest. "Why?"

"She's acting so strangely."

"So what's new? She always acts strangely. She's a free spirit."

Ruthie remained somber. "As we speak, she's at church."

"So?"

"It's Tuesday."

"What? People only go to worship on Sunday?"

She slapped the yearbook on the table. "She thinks she's Madonna. And there's the fishing thing."

Cara held up her hand to halt her. "*Fishing?*"

Ruthie sighed and reached across the table, patting Cara's hand. "You've been away for a while, honey. You'll see what I mean after a few days."

Cara turned her attention back to one of the boxes in front of her and pulled out a pair of white baby booties.

"Oh, were these mine?" she crooned, examining the tiny booties.

"No, dear. I made them for your children, just after you were born. Not that they'll ever be used," Ruthie quipped under her breath.

"You made booties for your own grandchildren when I was just a baby? What about me? What did I get to wear?" Cara shook her head in disbelief. Utterly bewildered, she stared blankly at the silk threads sewn in minute stitches with loving care. Her eyebrows furrowed as she read the name embroidered on the heels. "Omar? What's this Omar you have embroidered here?"

"Your grandmother made you plenty of booties when I was a little girl. I was merely passing on the tradition. One that I won't hold my breath you'll continue."

Oh, this vacation is going to be good, Cara thought. A full three weeks helping her parents get the house ready for sale, and listening to poor Ruthie's digs about her lack of grandchildren, was going to be a slow, agonizing death.

It was times like this she could throttle her brother for becoming a priest and dropping all the procreation pressure on her shoulders.

"And Omar," Ruthie continued, "is the name I picked out for your first born son. What can I say? I had a thing for *Dr. Zhivago.*"

"You were already naming my kids!? Omar?" She mouthed the name with disgust.

"You didn't like *Dr. Zhivago?*"

Cara drew in a deep cleansing breath of salted sea air, wondering how she could have been born to this crazy family. This was going to be an extremely long three weeks.

Ruthie plucked out an old birthday card from the box and read it. "Devin Michaels. Mmmm. Now that's a name I haven't heard you speak in a long time."

Turning it over, she read the ink staining the back and squealed in delight, practically jumping from her seat. "Devin proposed to you!"

"What are you talking about? He did not."

"On your birthday card. He proposed!" Ruthie sputtered, "How come you never told me about this?"

"Let me see that."

Cara nabbed the card from her mother and speed-read the note, smiling.

I, Devin Michaels, agree to marry you,
Cara Cavarlho should both of us still
be single at age thirty-five.
    Signed: Devin Michaels

"I remember this," she said as the memories poured back one by one. She and Devin had just toasted her birthday. After sneaking out on her own birthday party, they had sat on the concrete ledge of the watchtower at Gooseberry Point, watching the midnight moon, drinking cheap wine illegally, and toasting to their future success.

She had been lamenting about Manny leaving for the seminary and the predicament he'd left her with regarding her mother's future grandchildren. If she dared to remain single—which, given her lofty career goals, she'd whole-heartedly planned to be at age thirty-five—Ruthie was sure to hound her for the rest of her life. Or at least until menopause, whichever came first.

Devin joked that he would be chivalrous and rescue her from being eternally damned by her mother. What was nothing more than a little joke between two friends was now coming back to haunt her.

Cara couldn't help but smile, remembering the boy, the friend Devin had been. They'd been inseparable that summer.

"Devin always had a thing for you, you know." Ruthie raised her eyebrows and shined her matchmaking smile.

"Thirty-five seemed so old to us back then."

"Still is when you're single, dear," Ruthie returned.

Some things never change.

Cara rolled her eyes. "We were just kids, Ma."

Kids or not, back then they had thought they knew everything, most of all what they wanted in life. *Devin was going to take on the world,* she reflected. From the little bits and pieces she'd heard over the years from people back home, and news coverage on the tube of the highly publicized cases he'd won, he'd done just that, as a prominent Manhattan defense attorney. Winning one highly publicized case he'd taken straight out of law school, one that the prosecution as well as the world thought he would lose hands down, had propelled him into the most exclusive law firm in Manhattan. It hadn't taken him long to make a name for himself and become a much sought after, multi-million dollar man of law.

Cara had had her own plans, in which marriage had had no part. She had to admit pride in the fact that, like Devin, she'd reached the pre-set goals made that fateful summer. She had worked hard and become a home interiors expert, opening her own successful shop in the posh Back Bay area of Boston nearly ten years earlier.

Looking at her mother's bright expression, and knowing what conclusions she'd already drawn, Cara said, "It was a joke, Ma."

"It's in black and white."

"Blue and white."

"How many assistants have you lost to motherhood already?"

"Four."

"In a month or so, Louise will make five."

The heaviness of her mother's statement hit Cara hard, especially in light of the feelings she'd been having of late. Forcing the thoughts away, she tossed out the usual response she used when her mother started this line of conversation.

"That's why I'm not getting married. In case you hadn't heard, barefoot and pregnant went out long ago, Ma. Women have careers now."

"That may be so, but look me. I was so thrilled when you were born. I never once regretted leaving my catering business behind."

"My point exactly."

Ruthie scowled and snatched the card back, holding it to her chest as if it were the only hold she had on getting any future grandchildren. "We'll see about that. I may just get to see your father walk you down the aisle before I die after all."

Cara cocked her head to one side and blinked hard, trying her best to gather up her control. "I haven't heard from Devin in over fifteen years! I doubt he even remembers me."

Even as she said the words, she knew it wasn't true. She and Devin had been inseparable. Warmth spread from the center of her chest outward just thinking of their friendship. It had been a long time since she'd thought about Devin.

Ruthie gasped. "Don't be ridiculous! Devin would never forget you. If I know Devin, he'll keep his word. He'll honor this marriage contract," Ruthie continued, as if she were in her own world. "You must have some feelings for him or you wouldn't have kept his card all this time."

"I didn't even know it was there!"

"We'll see."

The way her mother clutched the card, fanning herself from mid-day August heat, Cara knew this was only the beginning.

Devin Michaels strode through the full glass door of his lavish downtown office in the heart of Manhattan, success evident from his steady gait.

"Congratulations, Mr. Michaels," the receptionist at the front desk said with a gleaming smile.

"Thank you, Lucy." He walked by the woman without so much as a nod of his head, ignoring the overt physical appraisal she made of him in his expensive suit as he strode down the corridor, leather briefcase in his hand. Despite his court win this morning, his mood had been growing more foul by the moment. If will alone could kill the bitter taste his profession left in his mouth, he'd have done it long ago. But the past few months of trying hadn't managed that feat.

"Way to go, Devin." Kurt Langdon, an associate partner, slapped him on the back, then shook his hand, squeezing it with competitive zeal. "They said it couldn't be won, but then again, you always prove them wrong. Victory is sweet, eh ol' boy?"

Devin glared at Kurt's hand on his shoulder until it was removed. He'd become used to the other lawyers in the office wanting to befriend him for the sole sake of furthering their own interests within Wallingford, Collins, and McCaid. Kurt's transparency made him nauseous. In fact, all of the vultures working in this firm were circling the dead flesh, waiting for their chance to have their name along with his.

Devin had made it his purpose to ensure his name alone would stand out before the rest. That's the way it had always been, and what he'd worked so hard for all these years. He didn't know when it had started, but lately he wondered why he had ever thought that was worth fighting for.

Kurt cleared his throat. "We're toasting the big win in the conference room in fifteen."

Devin nodded, then ventured toward his office door, hoping to find a quiet moment before he'd have to pretend to actually be happy he'd won a case where the guilty hadtriumphed.

"Congratulations, Mr. Michaels," Brenda said softly. His administrative assistant's soft brown eyes twinkled admiration up at him, and forced him to smile for the first time that day. They reminded him of warm cinnamon brown eyes that used to smile at him in his youth. Years stood in the way of those memories. Funny how ever since Brenda started working for him three months ago, those memories had kept creeping back into the recesses of his mind.

Brenda shuffled some papers on her desk and stacked them into a neat pile which she cradled in the crook of her arm. She was green out of business school, and although he had balked at the idea of taking on an assistant so inexperienced, she was quickly shaping up to be an asset to him. His reputation for being an arrogant barracuda was one that made it a difficult position to fill. Brenda's determination to keep up with him was something he admired.

He smiled his gratitude. "Thank you, Brenda."

She quickly grabbed her daily planner and steno pad, adding to the stack and followed on his heels through the double oak doors of his office. "You have a lunch meeting at noon with the senior partners. Mr. Ryan of Ryan Enterprises at two fifteen. Logan Hayward confirmed your squash game at three. You have a meeting with your Real Estate agent at four thirty to finalize the sale on your Co-op." She took a deep breath before continuing, her pause causing him to lift his head to look at her for the first time. "Dinner with Cheyenne at—"

"Cancel dinner," he cut in, remembering he'd forgotten to take care of that loose end himself. Cheyenne Lewis, his *companion* for the last six weeks when time permitted during his grueling schedule, had overstayed her welcome in his life. She was beginning to get too clingy.

"Send her flowers—I think she likes lilies—and tell her..." he thought a minute and shook his head. "I'm sure you'll think of something, but don't make any promises."

"Yes, Mr. Michaels," Brenda said, jotting the note in her steno. "Today's mail is on your desk as well as your phone messages. Ruth Cavarlho was insistent-"

Devin snapped his head up, his pulse quickening. "Who called?" He sucked in a deep breath as if the wind had been knocked out of him after hearing the name. When he saw his young assistant's startled expression, he realized his surprise was evident in the way he'd barked at her.

"Ruth Cavarlho," she repeated, darting her gaze from his face to her steno, her hand still poised in place for the next instruction. Then back again.

It wasn't like him to unravel in front of anyone. He'd be damned if he'd start today.

"That'll be all, Brenda," he said, straightening his spine and pushing strength into his voice as he spoke. A pen on his desk suddenly became his anchor and he gripped it between the pads of this fingers until Brenda nodded.

"Yes, Mr. Michaels." She turned and walked to the wide oak double doors and added, "They're toasting in-"

"Fifteen." He pushed up he suit jacket sleeve and glanced at the gleaming gold watch on his wrist. "Ten minutes. Call me. And get Ruthie Cavarlho on the phone for me, please."

The heavy door echoed in his head as it was closed. He sunk deep into his thick leather arm chair behind his desk and swung the seat around. Rubbing at his jaw, he stared out the window at the hustle and bustle of people below. Everything seemed so small. So very small.

For a man who'd made it his purpose in life to remain frozen, void of emotion, he was thawing fast. To feel anything at all would mean death in the snake pit of a career he'd willingly entered. It amazed him that the mere mention of a name, the thought of Cara could still trigger a deep emotional response. The years somehow hadn't managed to wash that away.

He leaned forward in his seat and rested his chin on his steepled fingers. The Manhattan skyline had always been a source of inspiration. It had been his dream. But lately, he'd been far too unsettled about the career that had always driven him hard. Instead of thrilling in the victory of a court case like this morning's win, his mind eagerly sought out memories of those easy summer days with Cara.

He remembered it well. It had been the summer before his father passed away. Carl Michaels had taken ill earlier that spring, told to get his affairs in order, and spend time with his family. The elder Michaels had never been willing to take time for anything other than activities he suspected would further his business interest. When they'd received the news his condition was terminal, the family had rented the same beach house on the coast of Westport, Massachusetts they'd always spent summers, hoping to capture years of what they missed in what little time they had left.

Before that summer, Devin hadn't even known his father, and when they'd finally had a chance to connect, he had lost him.

A bittersweet grin tugged at his lips. Although they were polar opposites in the looks department, he was a lot like his father.

Cara had been more than a friend. She'd been his rock, the one thing that he could always count on to keep him stable while the earth beneath him crumbled. When he had first seen her, he had been instantly attracted to her cinnamon brown eyes and chestnut curls. The coral string bikini she'd worn hadn't been half bad, either, he recalled, thinking of her walking along the shore collecting shells, flaunting assets she hadn't yet discovered a man found so desirable.

But it was friendship that had bound them together. It hadn't taken long for her laughter to embrace him and, eventually, they'd become inseparable.

Devin chuckled at the irony. He'd built his reputation being a hard as nails cut throat defense attorney. Respected and admired by his peers, he was feared by his opponents. Yet in one fell swoop, seventeen year old memories flooded him and brought him to his knees like a spineless jelly-fish.

The buzzer on his telephone sounded and Devin swung around in his chair to answer the page from Brenda.

"Mrs. Cavarlho on line one," she announced.

His heart raced as his pushed the blinking yellow light on the phone panel. Ruthie Cavarlho. Everything he remembered about her spoke of love and warmth.

"Devin, dear. It's so good to hear your voice," Ruthie said brightly.

"It's been a long time. I hope everything is well with you." *And Cara. Tell me everything about Cara*, he said inwardly. Look at him! He was shaking in his shoes like an eighteen year old boy pumped full of testo-sterone. If only the vultures outside his office door could see this...

"Yes. How's your mother doing, dear? It's been a few years since I've seen her. She doesn't come to Westport any more." Ruthie continued her small talk and filled Devin in on the family's plans to move to Florida within the month.

"I'm sure Harold is happy to be retiring." With a brisk motion, he slicked back his hair in frustration, waiting for her to be the one to men-tion Cara's name. A hot fire burned in his gut as he waited, anticipating the news that she was married, maybe with children, living happily ever after in the arms of another man.

But no, what was he thinking? That wasn't Cara at all. The Cara of his memory was a carbon copy of himself, driven in her quest for success. She'd chanted over and over again how she'd never marry. But that had been a long time ago...

"Did you receive Cara's card in the mail, yet?" Ruthie said, mention-ing her daughter for the first time.

He quickly rummaged through the stack of mail on his desk, tossing each letter aside until he found the thick violet enveloped. "I'm just read-ing it now." He tore the seal and pulled the cards—yes there were two, he noticed—and began to read the first.

Happy Birthday, Dev!

It's payup time!

Love, Cara

Confused, he glimpsed the second card, finding it vaguely familiar, and laughed out loud when he finished reading the back. Lord, it felt great to laugh. "I can't believe she kept this!" A strange feeling tugged at his heart that she'd kept a keepsake of him.

"Well, you know, Devin, she always had a thing for you," Ruthie confided as if it was a known fact among them all.

"How is she doing?"

"Fine."

He paused a second, a tinge of disappointment settling in his gut with her lack of elaboration.

"Good."

There was a slight pause before she continued. "She's staying at home until Labor Day, helping her father and me with the move and all. We're having a bit of a bash for her thirty-fifth birthday. We'd love to have you. Are you *available?*"

The inflection in her voice rose as to emphasize her double meaning. *Same ol' Ruthie.*

It wasn't until faced with the possibility of seeing Cara again that Devin realized he'd give anything to see her. He punched up his schedule on the computer and immediately groaned at entries flooding each and every day for the next month. "Things don't look good, Ruthie. I'm not sure I can get away."

"Oh, but...what about the wedding?" she gasped.

"Whose wedding?"

"Why...yours and Cara's, of course. You did read the card, didn't you?"

"Yes, but..." Puzzled by her query, Devin picked up the card again and turned it over in case he'd missed some important piece of information. The search proved futile.

"Cara will be thirty-five next week."

"Yes, I know."

"Well, then you know what that means, don't you?"

He was silent.

"Do you or don't you intend to honor that contract, young man."

A grin tugged at his lips. Although Ruthie's voice held a hint of amusement, he sensed her taking this line of offense immensely serious.

Knowing in advance how Ruthie Cavarlho operated, he proceeded with caution. "Ruthie, this *contract* is bogus. There was no serious intention of marriage by either of us, no meeting of the minds. No-"

"Devin, dear, don't talk to me in legal mumbo jumbo. I don't understand a word of it."

"It was a joke. It's not legal."

"Not legal," Ruthie grunted.

There was silence on the other end of the line for a few seconds. Devin picked up the ball point pen he'd strangled earlier and started tapping in his desk to fill in the void.

"Would Cara know this?" Ruthie finally asked.

"Well, I-"

"I'll bet she doesn't," she proclaimed, an undertone of hope resonating in her words. He could almost hear the wheels in her head spinning triumphantly when she declared, "What she doesn't know won't hurt her."

"Ruthie, what are you up to?"

"Nothing. I'm merely planning a birthday party for my single daughter, and I would love for you to attend. Is there anything wrong with that?"

"Of course not."

"And once you're here, if things should happen to, how shall we say, fall into place, then so be it."

He had to laugh. It surprised him how good it felt inside. He'd always been a sucker for Ruthie's charm, and seventeen years of passing time had made no difference.

"Devin Michaels, you know how fond I am of you. I've never made any bones about that," she admitted warmly. "And all these years I have been praying my daughter would someday find a nice man like you. So why can't it be *you*? I know you care for Cara."

He couldn't deny that. But it had never been the way Ruthie had always wanted. What he and Cara had shared was friendship, nothing more. His whole world with Cara felt like a lifetime ago. And at the same time, their friendship was so close to his heart he could almost touch it.

His heart pounded in his chest and he rubbed the spot that squeezed tight. "I'll see what I can do," he conceded, his smile fading. "But I can't make any promises."

"Be sure to bring your tuxedo."

He heard the phone click just as Brenda paged him again. "They're waiting for you in the conference room."

He cradled the phone in his palm wondering what the hell had just happened? He couldn't quite get a grip on the flood of emotions coursing through him. Dropping the phone, he fingered the pink slip on his desk with Ruthie Cavarlho's name scribbled on it for a good long time.

He wanted to see Cara. More than he could even think right now. There was a time when she had been the very first person—the only person—he'd seek out. She'd certainly seen him through the worst times in his life. And some of the best.

This was it, he realized. Going back to Westport to reconnect with his best friend was the medicine he needed help him get his life back on track.

Devin pressed the intercom button on the panel, suddenly feeling good for the first time in days. "Cancel," he said briskly, the rush of excitement from this morning's victorious court appearance long forgotten. The excitement of a new battle took its place.

"I...*I beg your pardon*."

"I said *cancel*! Make some excuse, I don't care what it is." Rubbing his face with his hand, he drew in a long breath. He couldn't believe he was actually considering something so foolish, so destructive, putting everything he'd work so hard for on the line.

All he had to do was make a few calls and he could catch the next flight. In a matter of hours he'd be standing face to face with Cara. Something inside him clicked, as if everything that was laid out before him no longer held any meaning. He knew what he had to do.

"Cancel the rest of the day, too. In fact, cancel the month. I'm taking a leave of absence starting now."

He heard Brenda's slight gasp. "Mr. Michaels, I don't understand-"

"Just do it! And Brenda, get me my Realtor—" His voice broke off, "No, never mind. I'll take care of that myself."

He leaned back in his chair and swung the seat around. Rubbing his chin between his thumb and index finger, he stared vacantly at the Manhattan skyline. The city he'd sought out in his youth, that drove him with every beat of his heart, had lost its magic with a single phone call. The unsettled feeling that had plagued him for the past few months suddenly lifted and he could finally breathe again. He was taking a new direction, and it felt great.

Hearing the buzz from Brenda again, he swung around and saw the light panel on his phone lit up like a Christmas tree. The grapevine in this office was as fast as a New York cabby racing from one green light to the next. He could almost hear the whispering vultures strategically planning his downfall outside his office door, starting with the moment he walked through it. And suddenly he didn't give a damn what they did.

Brenda sounded again with a repeated buzz that spoke of urgency. If he didn't make a quick getaway soon, the senior partners were sure to barrel through the doors of his office in fully justifiable protest.

Cara smiled grimly at the many people inspecting the odds and ends she and her family had accumulated her entire life and had displayed on their front lawn for purchase. She was annoyed, to say the least, at their perusal. This was her life they were scrutinizing!

When had she gotten so sentimental? Sure, her parents were moving away, selling the home she loved so much. But she'd left home long ago. Maybe it was just her time of the month. No, that would mean she had perpetual PMS for feeling the way she did. Who could possibly endure that?

Or maybe...it was because Roger, the man she'd been dating for the past year and a half, had become a fixture she wasn't sure she wanted in her life. She'd been a success in business, lived on her own in her Back Bay condo for the past few years. But this *thirty-five* thing was beginning to hit home.

She pushed the thought away, refusing to believe that her internal clock was waging war, and she was losing the battle.

"Is this real crystal?" a young woman—still a girl really—asked, holding the carafe Cara had given her mother as a birthday gift so many years ago. Her other arm was wrapped tightly around the waist of a young man. Amorous glances and giggles reflected the youth of their love. She wondered if they were newly married, filling their home with items they would some day put up for sale on their front lawn.

"Yes," she replied shortly, watching the young man. He had a familiar stand. It took her a moment, but she realized that he reminded her of a young Devin Michaels.

Funny. Ever since she found that damned birthday card, her mind wandered until it settled on Devin Michaels.

"We'll take it," the young man said, smiling affectionately at the girl. After digging through his wallet, he handed her the amount indicated on the little white tag Cara had so carefully placed on the bottle the previous evening. With their hands entwined, the young couple walked away.

That's when she thought caught a glimpse of him. *Devin Michaels*. She stood on the far side of the lawn, squinting her eyes from the sun to focus on the man sauntering through the open white picket gate. A dozen or so people had stopped and parked along the side of the road and were now leisurely waltzing across her parents pristine lawn.

The man could just as easily be someone who lived along the beach, just out for a stroll. She'd lived away from home so long that she'd lost touch with the comings and goings of neighbors. It couldn't possibly be Devin just because her mind suddenly wanted it to be. But as he ambled closer, she knew without a doubt it was Devin.

A glimmer of recognition registered on his face when he caught her eyes, and he mouth tilted to reveal a perfect smile. Her breath lodged in her throat, and she couldn't keep from feeling giddy. She nibbled on her bottom lip in an effort to compose herself.

The years had been good to him, she thought, noticing how the lanky boy he once was had filled out in all the right places. The man sauntering toward her now had wide shoulders and ripples along his chest, clearly visible beneath his polo shirt, a telltale sign that he spent time working out regularly. His charcoal eyes had deepened in color, giving off a masculine power of attraction that seared straight through her. It wasn't the Devin Michaels that she remembered from her youth, the shy but funny friend she'd teased so often. He was a man now. Powerful, stunning in movement and frightening with his dynamic presence all at the same time.

But he was still Devin Michael's, her childhood buddy.

"Devin," she said, catching her breath when he was finally standing before her. She looked up and noticed the inches he'd grown taller. He was now at least six inches taller than her five foot seven inch frame.

"Hello, *mia Cara*." The tender words rolled off his tongue with ease, sounding as soothing as the ocean that lulled her to sleep at night. *My dear one* was the meaning. Her grandmother had referred to her that way on countless occasions in her youth, which Devin had teased her about when he'd been privy to hear. But this time, the pure emotion with which he spoke the simple words cascaded over her like the incoming tide.

Chapter Two

Cara knew the face. She knew the name. But, for sure, she did not know this man standing in front of her. Brushing her sweaty palms on the sides of her jeans, she turned away from his probing gaze, not believing her eyes. When she turned back and blinked, she knew it was true. Devin Michaels was definitely standing in front of her in the flesh.

What was he doing back here after all this time?

She opened her mouth to speak, but the words somehow got lodged in her throat.

His deep rumbling chuckle made her glance up at him.

"What's so funny?"

He shook his head slightly and kept his eyes focused on her. "Nothing," he said.

She knew he was lying. He was teasing her for actually blushing, when she'd always been the one to tease him. She also saw that hidden beneath that scrupulously constructed veneer he held up like a shield, allowing the world only to glimpse the dynamic man that he'd become, he was the same Devin she remembered.

She couldn't help but laugh herself. "I can't believe you're really here."

"Me, too."

He brushed his hand over his head, passed the flecks of gray peppering the dark hair at his temples, until his hand settled at the nape of his neck. He'd gotten older. So had she. They weren't teenagers anymore.

She'd thought about him often over the years, meant to drop him a card or a phone call, but then got buried in whatever crisis needed her attention at the time. In the past few days, he'd been on her mind constantly. But until now, until she actually saw him in front of her now, she hadn't realized just how much she truly missed having him in her life.

Part of her had the most incredible urge to run to Devin and give him a great big bear hug. But this Devin was different than the boy she remembered. He was a dynamic man, and the awkwardness of seeing him this way made him seem like a stranger. She kept her distance with the table of salable trinkets wedged between them.

"It's good to see you, Dev."

"You, too." His dark eyes twinkled ever so slightly as to lift his shield an inch or two, giving her access to her old friend. He was still there. The same old Devin she'd know.

He opened his arms wide. "Come here. This one is way overdue."

A few quick strides around the table and he was by her side and then into her arms. His embrace filled her with tender feelings that brought her back in time, oddly comforting and unfamiliar at the same time. Cara ignored her foreign feelings and sank into his hard chest, reveling in the warmth his touch gave her. Cara forced a deep breath of salted sea air past the lump forming in her throat.

She'd lingered in Devin's arms longer than felt appropriate, and she pulled away, awkwardness taking over from the initial excitement of seeing him.

"So. What brings you back here? I thought your mom was still living in Connecticut, so it can't be family. Don't tell me you're tired of the Big Apple already?"

He shrugged slightly. "Well, actually...it was you."

Cara blinked. "Me? I don't understand."

"I got your birthday card."

She squinted an eye and gave him a teasing side long glance. "Not that I'm not flattered, that is, but you had to come all the way to Westport to thank me for a birthday card?"

He opened his mouth to speak but his voice was drowned out by a high-pitched squeal.

"Devin!"

Ruthie stood on the porch steps, frantically waving the kitchen towel she held in hand. "I'm so pleased you were able to make it!"

Cara looked up at Devin's suddenly suspect grin. "Make it? What's she talking about?"

Devin greeted Ruthie with a kiss on the cheek and a hug to Ruthie's utter delight. "You know I could never resist you, Ruthie."

Cara rolled her eyes to the sky, finally seeing the picture painted before her, one she was sure her mother artistically created.

"Mother, what have you done?"

Devin draped his arm across Cara's shoulders. "Don't be angry with her. I wouldn't have missed your birthday party for anything."

"Whose birthday party? I'm not having a birthday party."

"You're just in time, Devin. I have a lemon meringue pie cooling. I baked it just for you," Ruthie said, ignoring Cara's questioning gaze.

"You're having a birthday party for me?" Cara asked, looking at both of them, apparently the only one in the triangle who was completely clueless.

Devin darted a glance at Ruthie. "Did I just give something away?"

Ruthie waved him off. "Of course not. It isn't a surprise."

"Then why didn't you tell me you were having a birthday party?" Cara asked.

"I meant to but it must have slipped my mind," Ruthie said more innocently, backing up a step toward the porch. "You will be coming to dinner, won't you, Devin?"

"Of course. But..." he said to Ruthie, then looked back at Cara.

Cara searched his face for a second and saw no trace of amusement, just a bewilderment that seemed to match her own. Without a doubt, she knew Mother Ruthie was up to her old tricks again.

Ruthie stood on the steps of the porch now and clapped her hands together wildly. "Everything is going to be such fun now that you're here, Devin."

Cara glared at her mother and then turned her whole body to face Devin, trying her best to keep in control. "Oh, I'm sure it is. Help me out, Dev. What is actually going on here?"

"Ruthie really didn't tell you I was coming to Massachusetts? She called right after I got your cards."

"Cards?" Cara turned on her heels and gaped at Ruthie. Ruthie, in turn, gazed up at the bright blue sky, avoiding Cara's accusing stare. "I sent one card."

Ruthie backed up until she reached the last step of the porch and put her hand to her ear. "Is that your father calling me?"

"Daddy's at the hardware store and you know it," Cara returned.

"Then I think it must be the timer on the oven. I'll be right back."

Ruthie retreated into the house, the screen door slamming behind her. How many times had Cara been yelled at as a child for doing that very same thing?

Heat filled her cheeks for the second time that day as she gave Devin a sheepish grin. "Well, Dev, as you can see, some things never change around here. Sorry you were railroaded into coming. I'm sure she laid the guilt on thick."

"I wasn't railroaded. Ruthie invited me to your birthday party and I decided to come and visit." He laughed. "She hasn't changed a bit."

Cara sputtered, "Oh, you'd be surprised."

She hooked her arms around his waist and drew in the seductive scent of his musky aftershave. She didn't ever remember a time when she would have noticed such a thing in Devin. He'd always been her buddy.

"Well, I'm glad you came, for whatever the reason. How long are you staying?"

"I'm not quite sure. The whole trip was spur of the moment."

"I'm surprised you could get away on such short notice with your schedule. Or has my mother had this planned for a long time?"

"She just called me a few days ago."

She cleared her throat when an elderly couple came over to the table and started lifting and putting down trinkets that were on display. "Uh...where are you staying while you're here?"

He pointed back toward the beach. "Believe it or not, I was able to rent the cottage we use to stay at every summer before..." He broke off and shrugged uncomfortably.

Cara knew immediately what Devin was thinking about. "Before your dad...yeah, I know." She hadn't there to help him through the days just after his father funeral. She'd wanted to be there, but when his Dad took a turn for the worse, the family thought it was best to bring him home to Connecticut. She had called several times a day, talking to him for only brief moments as he had held vigil at his father's bedside. She had known he needed that time and hadn't wanted to intrude.

She'd stood beside him at the funeral and tried her best to give him some semblance of comfort in those difficult days. She had called from college to see how he was doing only to that Devin had already left for college immediately following the funeral. Although they'd written an occasional letter back and forth for a few years after that, life had omehow got in the way of their close friendship, and they had drifted apart.

"Ruthie sounds excited about the move to Florida," he said, changing the subject.

Cara groaned. "Yeah, that's why I'm here. You can't believe how much stuff has accumulated in this house. We've already made three trips to Goodwill and I don't know how many to the dump."

He looked straight at her, as if he was reading her mind. "You always did love this place. How are you doing with the move?"

She puffed her cheeks. Her first thought was to keep a stiff upper lip, but that would be ridiculous. Devin had always been able to read her. As he looked at her with the same caring expression she remembered so vividly from years before, she realized things were no different now.

"I don't know." She swallowed hard to fight back the sudden flow of emotion choking her. "It's really great to see you."

Devin bent forward, kissing her lightly on the forehead and she breathed in the scent of him, stirring her. He gave a quick glance around the yard. "Do you need to be here for this or can you get away for a bit?"

Ruthie poked her head out the kitchen window just as Cara was about to answer. "Go ahead, dear. I'm all set."

They both turned to face Ruthie.

Reaching back into the house, she clumsily forced a straw broom through the opened window and shook it violently. "I wasn't eavesdropping. I was...er...shaking out the broom."

Cara rolled her eyes, but she couldn't help but laugh. "Subtle is her middle name. Did I ever tell you that?"

"It's coming back to me."

The sun was still high in the sky as they took the old path down to the jetty where they used to sit and talk for hours. Cara had walked this path alone many time since, but something vaguely comforting kept coming to mind as they walked today.

She bent down and picked up a broken shell before tossing it back to the sand. "I still can't believe it's been seventeen years since we've walked along this beach together."

"There was an eagle nesting on that cliff over there that last summer, wasn't there," Devin said, pointing to a jagged ridge of rocks beyond the beach.

"I remember."

Cara plopped down onto the warm sand and discarded her sandals before burying her toes in the coolness below the surface of the sand. She threw her head back, resting with her arms behind her, letting the sun seep into her skin and the music of the ocean fill her head.

Devin sucked in a deep breath as he set himself down on the sand next to Cara. She was much more beautiful than he remembered because now she was no longer a girl, she was a woman. Her chestnut curls flowed freely down her back to the point of touching the sand and her creamy skin was as luminous as the sun. As they had the day he met her, her cinnamon eyes stopped him dead in his tracks. As a woman, she'd become refined, but he could still see a hint of her untamed beauty beneath her polished surface.

She lifted her head and turned to him. "You know, I saw you on CNN a few times."

He actually felt heat creep up his face. *Now that was a first.*

Cara jabbed him in the ribs teasingly. "Come on. Tell me you don't eat up all that press."

"It gives my mother bragging material when she goes to church bingo."

Cara laughed that wonderful way he remembered, her nose crinkling at the bridge.

"So, tell me, what was in the other card my mother send you?"

"Do you really want to know?"

Cara made a face.

"That little marriage contract I scribbled on your birthday card for your eighteenth birthday."

She shook her head and sputtered, "I knew she'd try something. No doubt Mom commandeered my birthday card to you and added her own personal touch."

Sitting forward, Cara began sifting sand through her long fingers. A stray lock of chestnut curls fell forward, framing her smooth tanned face.

"So what was it? You might as well tell me because I'll never get the truth out of her."

He grinned. "It's pay up time."

Cara sputtered. "Figures. I knew I got off way too easy when she found it."

"*She* found it?" He didn't know why that felt like a sudden jab to his heart. For the past couple of days, he'd been thinking it had been Cara who had searched him out, despite the fact that Ruthie had been the one to call. He'd been thinking of Cara for months, and naturally assumed she'd been thinking of him too when he had seen the card. Obviously, he had been wrong.

But what difference did it make? He was here now, and that was all that really mattered.

"We were rummaging through some old boxes, getting ready for the tag sale. She has still has this crazy notion that after all these years, you and I should get married."

"That's pretty much what she told me, too."

Cara sobered and flashed him a coy grin. "Is that really what she said?"

"Basically."

"I'm sorry, Dev. I'm sure the last thing you expected was to be pulled here by my mother's wild ideas."

"Don't be sorry. Actually, Ruthie's call couldn't have come at a better time. It provided me with a reason to get away from my office."

"I figured you'd be in high demand in Manhattan. Heck, after the way CNN went on about the *Great Devin Michaels,* I'd think you'd be booked with cases for the next ten or twenty years."

Sadly, it had been coming to that. Not that he was booked for the rest of the decade, but far enough in advance that he'd come to major blows with the senior partners for taking an indeterminate amount of leave. Every time he looked at that never-ending road ahead of him, all he wanted to do was turn back, forge his own path.

He glanced up at Cara and saw her probing brown eyes searching his face. He'd been right to come home to Westport. He needed clarity in his life, and this was exactly the place he could get it.

"Nothing that a few days of R and R can't handle. Like I said, I was glad when Ruthie called and gave me a reason to get away," he said, brushing off her concerned look. He didn't want to delve too deeply into the dark feelings he'd been having about his chosen career. He was just too damned happy to be there, talking with Cara like they always had, to think about anything else. There was plenty of time for soul-searching over the next few days.

She didn't press him any further, to his great relief. But the tightness in her brow as she gazed out at the ocean told him she was still thinking about what he'd said.

"So what about you? Your mother was pretty persistent. Any marriage plans you should be telling me about?" he teased, knowing he'd get a good rise out of her. He wasn't disappointed.

"Don't you start, too."

He laughed. "Has she always been like this? I mean, the whole time?"

Cara puffed her cheeks. "Not really. There were those few months in my mid-twenties when I was seeing someone she actually liked. I don't think she wanted to jinx anything, so she kept quiet. But once I hit thirty..." She whistled and pointed her hand towards the sand.

"Pretty much down hill from there?"

"You got it!"

Her expression changed slightly as a flash of pain cross her face. And then it was gone and she was smiling again.

"You know what I've been up against my whole life! I just found out the other day she has been making baby clothes for my future children since I was a baby myself. Does that sound normal to you?"

"Do you still feel the same about marriage and children?" he asked. He expected to hear a resounding "yes" as her answer, but to his surprise, she didn't.

Shrugging, she said, "So much is changing all around me, I don't know what to think."

He pulled himself up from the sand and extended his hand to help Cara to her feet. "Come on. Let's walk to the jetty. Surely that hasn't changed."

They walked a few moments in silence except for the distant sound of laughter on the far side of the beach and the roar of the waves rolling into shore. Devin couldn't help but think there was something more buried under the surface of Cara's control. The years had mellowed her a great deal. But it amazed him how he could still read her at all after all this time apart.

They trudged along the sand, virtually alone on the private beach except for some scattered beachcombers. More than once he'd stolen a glance in Cara's direction, only to find she was staring at him. God, how he had missed those brown eyes.

When he'd first hired Brenda to be his assistant, he had noticed her soft brown eyes and immediately thought of Cara. They'd haunted him ever since. Not Brenda's, but the memory of Cara's cinnamon eyes twinkling laughter up at him just like they were now, leaving him with a dead feeling inside for what he was missing.

As they reached the jetty, he reached for Cara's small hand and helped her onto the first boulder. Together they balanced themselves, jumping from one massive rock to the next until they reached the jetty's point.

Cara plopped down on a boulder, smooth from years of the incoming tide, and sat cross-legged.

"I think my mom has been pushing me harder these days because she doesn't want me to be alone when they move to Florida."

"What do you expect? She loves you."

"Yes, she does. And despite her crazy ways, I love her. But I'm nothing like her. She is the epitome of domestic life. I can barely fry an egg."

Devin lifted one knee and rested his arm across it as he sat on the boulder next to Cara. "Manny isn't around to keep tabs on you, and your parents are going to be a few thousand miles away. Can you blame your mother for wanting someone to watch over you?"

She laughed wryly. "I'm a big girl, in case you hadn't noticed."

"Yeah, I noticed." Much more than he cared to admit at the moment. So much about the two of them sitting together, talking, made it seem as if the seventeen years apart never happened.

And yet, feeling the heat from Cara's body, seeing the sun bouncing off the waves of her chestnut hair, he felt like he was seeing this incredibly beautiful woman for the first time. He was sure she'd been just as beautiful seventeen years ago, but somehow, he'd forgotten that part of her. He snapped his gaze out to the bay and stared at a bobbing sailboat coming into shore.

"Besides, I won't be alone. I have friends. And Roger will still be here."

Devin twisted himself around. "Who's Roger?"

He didn't realize his mouth had dropped open until he saw a full-blown smile stretch her incredibly delightful lips. "Ma didn't tell you about Roger, did she?"

"No."

Cara rolled her eyes and looked away. "Figures."

Ruthie hadn't once mentioned another man in Cara's life during their phone conversation. But now he wanted—no, needed—to know who this Roger guy was.

"I'm sure it was unintentional."

"Want to bet? I've been with Roger almost two years and they haven't been able to put up with each other for more than five minutes the whole time. I'll bet Ma didn't even invite him to my birthday party."

Devin chuckled. "Two years, huh? I've never made it beyond two months, but then I've never been one for longevity in the relationship department."

"Well, to mom, it's been two years too long. Roger is just as bad. He's thrilled beyond belief that my parents are moving to Florida. The further away the better."

She fiddled with a seashell that was imbedded in a crack in the boulder until it came free, then tossed it into the surf.

Cara hadn't said she was in love with the man. She'd merely said *involved*. A woman in love would be betrayed by the emotion in her eyes, no matter what words she spoke. He was deftly accurate at reading emotion, however fleeting, in the eyes of people under question, whether it be a potential client, a juror, the prosecution, or a woman in love. Since he saw no emotion cross Cara's face when she mentioned Roger by name, he could only surmise that she no longer was in love with him. If she ever was at all.

She drew in a deep breath and looked out at the white caps rolling in.

"The holidays must have been lively around here."

Cara rolled her eyes."You have no idea."

She was smiling again. Not just her mouth but her whole face. Her eyes lit up like fire flies on a hot August night, and her high cheekbones, delicately colored by the sun, brought back warm memories. In the sunlight, he could see the sheen of moisture that filled her eyes. "I've really missed this. Just you and me talking like this."

He had, too. He just hadn't realized how much until that moment.

"Me, too."

Reaching out, he touched her hand, stroking the soft flesh with his thumb. A whirl of heat spread through him like wildfire. He took in a deep breath and pulled his hand away, uneasy with this new-found emotion gripping him.

He'd been right to come here, no matter what the cost to his career. It was what he needed. From the few moments he'd just shared with Cara, he knew she needed it too.

"We should be getting back."

He just nodded. Then in a lighthearted tone, he said, "Go easy on your mother."

Cara quirked an eyebrow and gave him a wicked grin. "Like she's been easy on me? What do you take me for, Devin?"

Glancing over his shoulder at a couple of beachcombers, he did a double-take. In the distance was what looked like an elderly couple stripping their clothes. "We'd better head out now. It looks like they're about to turn this public beach into a nude beach."

"Huh?" She glance in the direction he'd motioned to, but the couple had already made it to the water and submerged. "It's kind of early in the day for skinny dipping, but it's probably one of the locals who live along the beach."

The sound of laughter had them turning around just as they jumped off the last boulder onto the sandy beach. Cara gasped and focused her attention on the nude couple dropping to the sand.

Her hands flew to her mouth. "That's no ordinary blue-haired lady!"

"Who is it?"

Her face was as white as a sheet. "That's my *grandmother*!"

An hour later, Devin was sitting at the small harvest kitchen table, dipping his spoon into a delectable bowl of Ruthie's famous lemon meringue pie. Cara had excused herself to make a phone call.

"You've outdone yourself, Ruthie," Devin said, taking the last bite.

Ruthie smiled her pleasure and lifted the bowl, silently offering another slice of pie.

"Maybe later," he replied, gesturing with his hand to his stomach.

"There's plenty left for after dinner. I have some nice steaks from the butcher marinating as we speak."

Ruthie moved about the kitchen, putting pots and pans in the white cabinets, and wiping the counter of spills that weren't there. The radiant smile on her face made it clear she was enjoying the "mess" she'd created for her daughter, and she made no bones about hiding it.

"You're so transparent, Ruthie," he finally said.

"Am I?"

"You asked me to come here to break up Cara and her boyfriend, didn't you?"

She grunted under her breath. "She told you about him, then."

"You don't like him?"

She stopped cleaning her already clean surfaces and turned to face him, leaning her hip against the counter by the sink. "He's...*fine*," she said tersely.

Fine. No elaboration. He was going to have to pry it out of her. He was good at that. He used the one thing he was sure would get a rise out of her and make her reveal all. "I'm sure that it's just a matter of time before they marry and she gets pregnant with-"

"Over my dead body! And that won't be any time soon, mind you." Pointing a finger at him, she added, "If I have my way, there will be no marriage between Cara and Roger."

As crazy as Cara had always gotten about her mother's antics, Ruthie had always been a good judge of character, just the kind of person he could have used in the courtroom to review a panel of jurors. If she had some beef with Roger, then she had to have had a good reason. Otherwise, why waste time calling a man in Manhattan that her daughter hadn't seen in years when Cara could easily have given her plenty of grandchildren with this Roger guy.

"He's not a bad guy, is he?" he asked. An ominous thought crept into his mind, causing his heart to pound in his chest. "He doesn't hurt her, does he?" *He'd kill the bastard.*

She shook her head and waved a hand at him. "No, no. Nothing like that. Roger is a perfectly *fine* gentleman." She breathed a heavy sigh. "He's just not you."

He had to laugh at that. "She's a grown woman, Ruthie. She has a right to choose whomever she wants to spend her life with."

"Not if she's choosing wrongly."

"And you think she is?"

"Roger is the kind of man a woman chooses when she wants stability."

"There's nothing wrong with stability."

"He is not marriage material, and he is certainly not the man who will be the father of my grandchildren."

There was definitely something deep beneath the surface of Cara's relationship with Roger. But Ruthie went back to polishing already-clean surfaces, leaving Devin to wonder just what this *fine* Roger was all about.

"Don't you think you're being a bit calculating where Cara is concerned? I mean, she is a very independent woman. She perfectly capable of taking care of herself," he said in Cara's defense.

Ruthie held her hand to her heart in mock exasperation. "Calculating? You wound me, Devin."

He smiled, knowing that Ruthie truly did not have a mean bone in her body. "Well, maybe calculating was a bit harsh. How about-"

"Concerned," Ruthie decided for him. "I'm concerned for the well-being of my daughter and my future grandchildren."

"But what about Cara? Doesn't she have a right to be with the man that *she* chooses?" he asked.

"Of course she does. That's my whole point." Ruthie threw her hands in the air as if the lightbulb she'd been trying to turn on finally illuminated. "She's already chosen him. She just doesn't know it yet."

Well, that was Ruthie for you, Devin thought with a wry grin. She had her own way of thinking about how the world revolved around the sun. Underlying her reasoning was a healthy dose of mother knows best. If he was going to be an ally for Cara, he had his work cut out for him.

Cara plopped on her bed and stretched for the telephone on the white wicker night-stand. Noting the time on her digital alarm clock, she took a deep breath and dialed Roger. After what she and Devin just witnessed on the beach, she wasn't sure if she was ready for the next plunge on this rollercoaster ride of a vacation.

Roger answered on the first ring. "Good afternoon, Roger-" he began, his usual spiel, but Cara cut him off.

"It's me, Roger." She hoped she hadn't got him in the middle of something. But that was ridiculous because he was always in the middle of something. The last time she'd interrupted him while he had been working at home, he had practically bitten her head off about consideration. "I didn't pull you from a huge tax return, did I?"

His voice was strained with patience, giving her the answer. "How is the beach?"

"Good. The same."

"And Mother Dearest?"

"She hates it when you call her that."

Roger chuckled. "I know. But she hates me, period, so we're even."

Cara rolled onto her back and stretched out on the floral down comforter, letting her legs dangle over the side. "Unfortunately, I fit into this equation, so it's not exactly even."

"Are you coming back to Boston?" he asked, a hint of optimism coloring his tone.

"No. I still plan on staying until Labor Day." She cleared her throat before asking her next question, and steeled herself for the battle to come. "I was hoping you could get away for a few days and come down here."

Silence.

"Roger?"

She heard his sigh carry over the phoneline. "You know how I feel about visiting your family."

"Yes, but it's me, too. It'll be three weeks until I'm home. Aren't you going to miss me?"

"Westport is not that far from Boston. You could drive up for dinner, stay overnight. They don't have you locked in your room, do they?"

Cara stiffened. It was a losing battle to expect Roger to willingly come down to her parents' beach home and enjoy it. He'd never stayed more than a few hours at a time, and the animosity had flowed freely between Roger and her mother. "My parents are having a birthday party for me. Did you know anything about that?"

She heard the exaggerated breath carry over the line again and figured he'd probably been purposely excluded. She have to fix that with her mother later. His reply, however, was much softer than she'd anticipated. "No. But I was hoping we could have a more private celebration, like say, at the Bay Tower?"

She wiped the sweat from her forehead with the back of her hand. "That's sounds romantic. Maybe we can do that when I get home. I want to introduce you to an old friend that's back in town for the party."

"Oh? Have you ever mentioned her before?"

She tried to act nonchalant. "No. His name is Devin Michaels."

"If you have an old friend to spend some time with, what do you need me there for?"

Her heart fell with his response. Okay, not so much his actual words, she realized, but his tone. There wasn't an ounce of jealousy flowing through this man's veins. She'd never thought of herself as the kind of woman who'd enjoy the trappings of a relationship. It was one of the reasons she never wanted to marry. But with Roger, everything was open. He'd never felt any kind of threat that another man might steal her attention away. For once, she wished he'd let down his almighty guard and show a little emotion.

Normally it wouldn't have meant so much to have Roger around. Although their relationship had been steady, they definitely weren't joined at the hip. But ever since this afternoon when she had first seen Devin standing on the lawn, it was as if her equilibrium had been thrown off kilter. She couldn't deny the instant attraction she felt when Devin gazed at her with his dark eyes. It was magnetic, mystical almost, as if he could read her mind. She needed Roger there to keep herself grounded and keep the crazy emotions she'd been having at bay.

"I'm not going to spend all my time with Devin. Besides, we'd talked about taking the ferry to Nantucket a few times and never got around to it. Now's our chance."

"It means that much to you?"

"Yes."

"Okay," he said in resignation. She could almost see him forcing a smile for her benefit. He would tolerate being at her parents', but he wasn't happy about it. But because it meant a lot to her, he'd come. "I'll be there early, before the rush hour traffic. But just so you know, I'm going to make it a working vacation."

She couldn't help but smile. "You can use Daddy's den. He's always at the hardware store, anyway."

Cara dropped the phone in the cradle and brushed back her hair with her fingers. It was going to be strange having Roger staying under the same roof as her family, eating at the same dinner table for more than just a few hours. Meeting Devin Michaels.

Was she nuts? What had she just got herself into?

Chapter Three

"Rise and shine, sleepyhead."

Cara moaned at the sound of Devin's voice. With her eyes still closed, she fought to keep from being pulled from the dream she'd been having.

The ground was moving around and around. The carnival music blared and the bright lights flashed all around them. *Up, down, up down.*The carousel horses danced in a row, the wind whipping through her long brown hair making it float on air like the mane of real stallion racing.

"Cara."

She turned to the sound of Devin's voice. He stood at the sidelines, calling her name. *Up, down, all around she moved, passed him.*

"Devin?"

The music began to die down. The horses moved in slow motion. When the carousel came round again, Devin was gone. In the distance she saw him, moving through the crowd. *He was leaving her.*

The ground beneath her began to rock.

"Cara? Wake up."

The bed rocked to and fro. Cara sucked in a deep breath, wanting the dream to stay alive, wanting to turn around and come back for her. *"Where are you going?"* she called out to him in her dream. But he didn't turn around. He was gone.

Cara's eyes flew open and when they did, she saw him. Devin was there, his broad shoulders hunched over her as he sat on the side of her bed, gazing into eyes. His strong hands were gripping her bare shoulders.

"You came back," she whispered in what sounded to her like a sleepy whimper.

His brows furrowed slightly. "I told you last night that I would."

Slightly dazed, Cara looked down, suddenly aware of where she was. And what she *wasn't* wearing. Although she was wearing her underwear and a light cotton tank top, the top was old and worn in all the wrong places. It was as good as wearing nothing at all in mixed company.

Devin pulled back and cleared his throat, looking almost apologetic. The heat in his eyes was unmistakable. "Ah...Ruthie. She suggested I come in and wake you."

In a groggy state, she clutched the white percale top sheet to her neck to cover her bareness. "I'll just bet she did."

No longer quite as sleepy, she gazed up at Devin and saw he was dressed in a tank top and running shorts. His smoky eyes smiled at her.

"What are you doing here so early?" she asked, glancing at the clock on the nightstand. It read six o'clock. "So ungodly early, I might add."

"We made plans last night to go jogging on the beach this morning. I told you I'd be here early. You still up for it?"

She rubbed at her gritty eyes and focused on him again and realized he was serious. She shifted in the bed and the thin sheet covering her pulled from her neck, revealing her bare shoulders and a little too much skin just above her breast. She hiked it back up to her chin.

"Yes, but for me that usually means after a cup of coffee and a shower at, oh, somewhere around nine o'clock?"

He raised his eyebrows. "Why so late?"

"That's still early for most people, Dev."

Chuckling, he added, "I sometimes forget that not everyone is a top-of-the morning person."

His expression turned sheepish. She remembered that well. It was one he'd always had when he was confessing some deep-seeded secret or dream he'd had as a kid. One he thought she'd find ridiculous. But she never did.

Devin sat on the bed beside her, looking suddenly very comfortable despite her bareness, as if finding her half naked in bed was somehow normal.

With increased awareness, vanity set in. She combed her fingers through her disheveled hair. "Yeah, well, I'm still a don't-look-at-me-until-after-coffee person." She motioned her head toward the bedroom door. "If Ma's up, you just may get lucky and get some breakfast."

"I'll meet you downstairs." He rose from the bed, causing it to shake, and turned toward the door. She didn't drop the sheet until he closed the door tightly behind him.

Her usual morning routine of showering and dressing was completed with record speed, despite the fact that on a normal morning, she would have downed two cups of coffee during the process. Twenty minutes later, she waltzed into the kitchen toward the smell of freshly brewed coffee to find her mother and Devin were nowhere in sight.

Her grandmother, Elsie, weighted down with more fishing gear than a person her size could possibly handle, was just passing through the kitchen when she walked in.

So this was the fishing thing her mother talked about.

"Gram, what are you doing?" she asked, almost feeling ridiculous for asking a question that should be so obvious by her attire.

"Can't talk now," Elsie said with a bright smile. "I'm late."

"Where are you going?"

"Cod fishing. I've got to go while the getting is good." She reached out and grasped the door handle, but Cara held her back.

"Please, just come and sit for a minute so we can talk."

"We can talk later. The fish are waiting."

Cara clutched her hands together, not sure how to proceed with the subject at hand. "What about the man I saw you with? Is he waiting, too?"

Elsie turned back quickly, frantically waving her hands back and forth to shush Cara. "Your mother will hear you."

Cara lowered her voice to match her grandmother's tone. "Ma doesn't know?"

"Of course not. Do you think I want her poking into my life the way she does yours?"

"Not possible. You're not in your child-bearing years."

Elsie sank into the kitchen chair, Half her gear rattled back and forth, hitting the table with her motion. "What's more important is how you know about Albert."

"Albert. I, uh, we saw you yesterday," she stammered. *Okay, how do you tell your nearly eighty-year old grandmother you saw her frolicking naked in the sun?* "Devin and I *saw* you."

"Devin?"

"You know, the man who was at dinner last night?"

"The accountant? Phooey! All accounts are shysters. Best to steer clear of him, dear. He'll only break your heart in the end." Elsie started to get up as if that was sufficient enough to explain her actions, but Cara gently pulled her back down.

"No, you remember Devin Michaels. He used to spend the summers in the cottage right up the beach."

As if a lightbulb had just been illuminated, her eyes widened and she nodded her head. "Oh, yes, he was a nice boy. How is he doing?"

Cara shook her head in frustration. "Grandma, you had dinner with him last night. Are you purposely trying to be evasive with me? Because that really only works with Ma."

Elsie sagged against the back of the chair and made a face. "I should have known I couldn't pull that past you." She gave a good belly-laugh, rattling her gear again. "You've always been too much like me. Drives your mother crazy."

But Cara wasn't laughing. "What's going on?"

"Albert is a nice *young* gentleman friend of mine," she said with a satisfied smile. The emphasis on the word "young" did not escape her.

Far be it for Cara to begrudge her grandmother happiness, but there was the bigger, more frightening issue of her behavior. "Ma thinks you have Alzheimer's."

"No. I have a life."

When that was the only response her grandmother offered, she elaborated. "Ma says you've been doing odd things, like saying you're going to church in the middle of the afternoon."

"I don't see anything wrong with that. Lots of people go to church every day."

"Yes, but you don't go, do you. I saw you...on the beach," Cara said delicately.

"You did?"

"You were with Albert."

Elsie's wrinkles deepened into a frown. "Were you spying on me?"

"No, I was taking a walk and saw you swimming in the nude." She hoped she wouldn't have to elaborate on the part that was too close to the love scene in *From Here to Eternity*. It had been hard enough to accept when she saw it.

"I think that Albert and I deserve to have a little bit of privacy, don't you?"

"Gram, you were naked on a public beach!"

Elsie balled her fist. "Dear, when life happens you have to grasp it and live it with gusto." She stood and shuffled to the door, making it clear that the conversation was over as far as she was concerned. With a bright smile, she added. "Have a nice day."

Cara buried her face in her hands and shook her head. Her poor mother thought her grandmother had Alzheimer's and all she was doing was having a torrid affair. She didn't know what bothered her more, the deception, or the fact that her grandmother was the *only* one having a torrid affair.

She took a deep breath and let the smell of coffee fill her head. A healthy dose of caffeine would do her some good. She paced across the green tiled floor and pulled a ceramic mug with little yellow daffodils on it from the cabinet. After preparing a cup for herself, she slumped back, leaning her hip against the counter, wondering where Devin had disappeared to.

Surely her mother would have jumped at the chance to make him breakfast. Ruthie was never so happy as when she was cooking for a hundred people.

A warm breeze floated lifted to the curtains and brought with it the sound of voices. Pushing back the sunflower curtains above the kitchen sink, she saw Devin on the front porch gripping a coffee mug in his hand as he leaned against the porch post. Her mother sat at the wrought iron table next to him, arranging a colorful bouquet of flowers in a painted ceramic vase. All she needed to hear was Roger's name and she knew she didn't want to go anywhere near that porch. Lord only knew what Ruthie was filling Devin's head with.

The familiar sound of the silver BMW pulling into the driveway pulled her attention away from the porch. She drew in a cleansing breath and pasted on a smile, readying herself for the upcoming storm. Roger was here.

He said he'd come, and like always, he was true to his word. That was a good trait in a man, she'd always told herself. She thought about the conversation she'd just had with her grandmother. Just once, Cara thought with regret, she'd like to trade some boring old predictability for a little bit of heavenly gusto.

Pushing through the screen door, Cara felt a surge of unease wash over her. Ruthie, in true form, was already scowling as Roger climbed out of the car and slammed the door. The uneasy feeling grew stronger and Cara vaguely wondered if this was how the people of Washington State had felt just before Mount Saint Helens had blown her top.

Devin slumped back against the porch railing, listening to the musical cry of seagulls on the beach as he watched the tall sandy-haired man step out of the car.

So this is the guy he'd just gotten an earful about.

Devin had just spent the last twenty minutes listening as Ruthie talk about "fine" Roger. From everything Ruthie had said, he was everything Cara would want in a man. He watched as the man smiled when Cara appeared in the doorway. His teeth were too straight and his hair was too neat. But Devin knew too well that appearances could be deceiving. *No one could be that perfect.*

Devin's eyes were drawn to Cara as she stepped out onto the porch. She was dressed in a crisp white T-shirt and navy skin-fitting spandex running pants which hugged her thighs. For a fleeting moment he imagined those thighs pressed firmly against his own body. He wonder just when those thighs had become that appealing.

His body responded as it had earlier when he had first caught sight of her in bed. Seeing her sleeping, with her wild dark hair cascading over her pillow, had pretty much drove him insane. An honorable man would have turned and walked away as soon as he opened the door and saw her curled up in a ball on her side. But there was nothing honorable about the way the sight of her, wearing a nothing night shirt, made him feel.

When he saw the white sheet draped loosely over her body, revealing smooth creamy skin only a lover should be privileged to enjoy, his whole body had kicked into overdrive. He had been pulled into the room like some mighty magnet drawing him to her. It had taken all the strength he had to cover her body and shield his eyes from the very vision that kept playing over and over in his mind now, driving him mad.

He fought to shrug off this animal need enveloping him as he looked over at Cara. Let's face it, friend or no friend, he still had a fairly strong male libido. He was a guy, after all, and Cara had turned into one incredibly desirable woman. It was only natural for him to respond to her. It would pass.

With a pensive smile, she climbed off the porch. "You said you'd be here early, but I had no idea you'd be up before the roosters, too."

She walked down the concrete path toward the driveway where Roger stood. He gave her a quick peck on the cheek, but it was clear that Cara expected more by the way she back away at his quick response to seeing her.

Although he and Ruthie were still on the porch and Roger and Cara were standing a good distance away in the driveway, Roger's voice carried to them with brilliant clarity. "So how's Ruthie dearest?"

Ruthie stiffened. Apparently she'd heard his brash remark, too. But ever the gracious hostess, Ruthie smiled and swung around to greet her new house guest. "So nice of you to drop by, Rupert," she said.

"The name is Roger," he corrected with a heaving sigh. "It's been a while."

"Yes, of course. Will you be staying for breakfast?" she asked brightly, although, by the way Ruthie stood straight as a board, Devin got the idea she'd like to pitch him out the door right now...or at least throw him to the wolves.

Cara's lips thinned. "I told you Roger was going to stay with us for a few days."

"Oh...how nice," Ruthie returned.

Cara stood at the end of the path, pleading with him with her eyes to help. Devin just grinned, the devil in him deciding it was much too fun to watch the flames.

"I'm Devin Michaels," he finally said, holding his hand out to shake Roger's.

"Cara mentioned she had an old friend in town," Roger said, advancing toward the house. "Good to meet you. I'm Roger Fine."

Devin coughed to hide his surprise.

"Are you okay?" Ruthie asked, shining an impish grin.

"Swallowed a bug." Devin gripped Roger's hand and was a little taken aback by the lack of force in his hold. In his profession, the handshake was a power struggle. If an opponent's grip was too soft, he immediately knew he had it in the bag. Too hard, and he was on equal ground. Devin never preferred the former. Being equally matched in and out of the courtroom always kept him on his toes. It wasn't that way with many of the other attorney's he knew, who opted for the easy way out. He tried hard to squash his gut feeling. Cara was dating a wimp.

"You look like you two are off for a run," Roger commented, looking at Cara's attire and pulling at the braid dangling down her back.

"Would you like to join us?" Devin asked. He couldn't help himself. A little healthy competition was good for everyone and he couldn't wait to see just was Roger was all about.

"Sure."

Cara did a double take, as if she hadn't heard him right. "But you've never gone running with me before."

"There's a first time for everything."

Cara smiled her pleasure. Clearly the simple gesture meant a lot to her and had Devin wondering more and more about this strange match.

"I'll just get my bags and change." Looking at Cara and Ruthie he added, "Where?"

"Why don't you take your bags up to Manny's old room. You'll have plenty of room in there."

Cara swung around to her mother. "That's not necessary. He can stay in my room with me. It's big enough for the two of us."

"Cara, I'm surprised at you. How would it look to your grandmother to have a man staying in your room? And you're not even married."

Devin wanted to laugh at the little dig and wondered how Ruthie would react to hearing about Elsie's attempt yesterday to turn a public beach into a nudist colony.

This was going to be good, he thought, crossing his arms across his chest. It was worth it to come to Massachusetts if only to see how this triangle would play out.

"Besides you only have a full-sized bed in your room. It's much too small for the both of you."

"I don't-" she started to say, but Roger held her back.

He blinked hard as if he were trying to hold back his own retort. Cara clenched her fists at her side.

"Manny's room is fine," Roger conceded. Then turning to Cara, he added, "I'll just change and meet you down here."

Cara nodded and folded her hands across her chest.

"I have to write up a list for your father to take to the hardware store today," Ruthie said before disappearing in the house behind Roger.

When they were alone on the walkway, Devin asked, "I thought you said your father was at the hardware store yesterday."

"He was."

"Then why is he going again today?"

"He only goes to watch the Red Sox game."

That may have been perfectly clear to her, but to him, it made absolutely no sense.

As if Cara had read his mind, she added. "Ma doesn't let Dad watch sports in the house anymore. She got sick of hearing him scream and yell when someone made a bad play."

"So he goes to the hardware store to see the game?"

"Right. That way, Ma doesn't have to listen to him scream, Dad gets to watch the game, and while he's there he picks up things he needs to fix the house."

"So everyone is happy."

She laughed that wonderful rich laugh and he knew he'd have come here for that reason alone. "You are the only one I know whose head doesn't spin when I talk about my family." She shook her head.

"Not like Roger, I gather."

Cocking her head to one side, she said, "You've been talking to my mother, I take it."

He shrugged. "She's concerned. You want to tell me your side?"

Cara rolled her head, then pulled her sweatband on her forehead. "There isn't enough time in a lifetime to tell you how my mother feels about Roger."

It was an odd feeling, watching Cara and Roger together as they ran along the sand. Devin had never considered himself a jealous man. There'd really never been a woman who'd made him care one way or the other. Indifference, that's what it was all about to him back in Manhattan. Women were merely a physical outlet for releasing pent-up frustration from the everyday grind. He made no promises and had no regrets.

He'd never been sexist enough to think a woman couldn't stand her own ground in a court of law. He even admired those who'd sometimes use their feminine wiles to their advantage while trying a case. It was only strategy and those same women knew when to back off. After all, every attorney had their strengths and weaknesses and they all played for the same prize. The win. Fortunately for him, he did most of the winning.

But now, he had to admit to being a bit green.

As they rounded the grassy bend for Gooseberry Point, Cara panted, "Race you to the watchtower, Michaels."

"Is that a challenge?"

"You bet."

He jogged in place and waited for Roger to catch up. When he did, Roger doubled over and rested his hands on his knees, his breathing was just short of a wheeze.

"What do you say, Rog. Are you up for it?"

Roger shook his head back and forth.

Cara stopped jogging, a note of concern etched her expression. "Maybe this wasn't a good idea. We could try walking for a while."

"No, no, you guys...go ahead. I'll catch up...with you."

She cast a questioning glance at Devin. "I don't know."

"Trying to get out of it already?" Devin teased.

She eyed Devin devishly and laughed. "You'd better hope you win."

"Like old times, I intend to."

Leaving Roger behind, they sprinted full force along the causeway leading to the Gooseberry Point watchtower. Although Devin had the advantage of longer legs and wider strides, he admired how Cara rose to the challenge and kept right up along side him.

As they reached the tower, he saw how the morning sun hitting the side of the gray stone tower made the shiny green ivy growing along the edge glisten. He avoided the rest of the greenery by staying on the walking path, although running through it would have given him the advantage.

Cara sprinted through the first-floor door first and ran up the center of the stairway, their footsteps echoing off the surrounding walls, with Devin just a step behind. The cooler air inside the stone watchtower was inviting and bathed him with each stride higher until he reached the top.

"Beat you," she panted, gripping the outer rail of the landing. She walked in circles, feathering back the wayward curls that had fallen loose from her braid.

Watching her do this brought Devin the most incredible urge to reach out and do it himself.

"You cheated," he said, following her lead and walking in circles to keep his muscles from stiffening.

"Did not. You're a sore loser."

"You're right, but you still cheated."

"How?" she said, raising her arms up and then dropping them to her sides.

He leaned against the rail, looking out at the ocean, trying to catch his breath. "I held the door open for you."

She shot him a side long glance. "So you lost on the side of chivalry? Try again, Dev."

He laughed.

"Besides, it was a piece of plywood, and all I did was seize the moment. You would've done the same thing."

"True enough. So what do I owe you for the win?"

She waved him off. "We didn't bet anything."

He pulled off the sweatband on his head. "So we'll bet now."

She thought about it a minute until her expression lit up. "The Portuguese Festival is in a few days. It would be a miracle to get Roger to go. He hates those things."

He frowned. "You mean, just the two of us? Wouldn't Roger be jealous of you spending the evening with another man?" He got the distinct feeling he would be where Cara was concerned.

She sputtered. "Roger doesn't have a jealous bone in his body. He'd probably be relieved I wasn't nagging him to go. You saw the pile of paperwork he brought with him, didn't you?"

Devin shrugged. "What's with you two?"

She didn't say anything for a minute and looked out into the bay, clearly uncomfortable with discussing her personal affairs. He didn't like that. They'd always been able to talk about everything. But then he had to remind himself that seventeen years lay dormant between them. She had a new best friend to share her hopes and dreams with. and had for quite some time.

And it wasn't him.

"Roger is a very kind person. We never argued. He's stable and predictable, everything a woman would look for in a husband, really."

"Except you."

She sighed, closing her and chuckling wryly. "I should want to marry him, shouldn't I?"

"Not necessarily. Some people just don't want marriage and family. You never did."

She shook her head. "That's not it. I should *want* to marry a man like Roger. He's hard-working, considerate, faithful. It's not like he's asked or anything. In fact, I don't think he'd ever consider it, and to be quite honest, I think that's part of the attraction."

"Then what is it?"

"God, I hate to admit this."

"Just blurt it out then. You got your best friend here, remember?" A warm smile lit up her face and his breath caught in his throat.

"Have you every looked at your life and thought, yeah, I have everything I have ever wanted. I've reached all my goals."

He nodded.

"But I want more. Life is changing. Everything around me is changing." Her hands flew to her face. "And now my biological clock is out of control."

His eyes flew open. He actually couldn't believe what he'd just heard. "A baby? You want a baby?"

When she pulled her hands away, he saw the unmistakable color that stained her cheeks. She was blushing as if she were almost embarrassed to admit it. Embarrassed!

"Not just a baby. I want a family of my own."

"You always said you never wanted kids."

"I know. Think how shocking this is for me to suddenly be getting the urges my mother has been hoping for."

She was laughing now and he couldn't help but laugh himself.

He thought about Cara as a mother. Yeah, he could see it, although until that moment he'd never thought of her as the motherly type. She'd always focused so much on her goals when they had been younger that it hadn't occurred to him to look past that.

"I've achieved every goal I've ever set for myself. I keep thinking, I've got a great life, a solid career, a wonderful condo and lots of friends." She reached around herself and hugged her middle. "But then my arms feel empty and every time I take a good look at what I have, I wonder if that is what I really want. Maybe I'm missing out on the best part of life. I believe that's family."

"And Roger doesn't want that?"

She blew out a quick breath and chuckled wryly. "Actually, we've never talked about it."

"Maybe you should be talking with him about this, instead of me."

She lowered her voice as if she were confessing some deep secret meant only for him to hear. "I don't know."

"If he's not all that keen on the idea you could always have a baby by yourself."

"Oooh, what you just said," she said, crinkling her nose as if she smelled something foul.

He hunched his shoulders. "What did I say?"

"Look at my family, and think about how that won't work." She splayed her fingers and began counting on them. "For one, my brother is a priest. For two, my mother would never let me hear the end of it no matter how much she wants grandchildren. And three," her face softened and her voice lowered, "I don't think that it's fair to expect a child to grow up without a father. Not if I can help it."

She had a point. More and more studies indicated the need for children to have an active father figure in their lives. He knew first-hand how hard it could be for a kid without a dad. He had a father, but he had never been around until it was too late. If Cara was seriously considering having a baby, she'd go the whole route and make sure her child had everything he or she needed in life. Including a full family with a real mom and dad.

"I've focused so long on myself and my career that I just don't know if I can do it. And certainly not alone. Sometimes I think I'm too selfish to be a mother."

Devin shook his head at the absurdity. "You're wrong." How could she think such a thing?

"Am I? As you discovered, I'm not a morning person. What if I get angry if the baby wakes me up? What kind of mother does that to her kids?" She sat on the concrete steps leading down and leaned forward, propping her elbows on her knees. "I don't want to bring a baby into my life only to discover it's too late for me to switch channels."

He watched her drawn expression. Clearly this was an issue she'd given some serious thought to, and now felt she was at a crossroads.

"It's never too late if it's what's really in your heart. You never know. It may be easier to talk to Roger about this than you think."

She gazed up at him and sighed. "I don't know. It's just so different with you, Devin. I mean it. It's actually easy to talk with you about whatever crazy feelings I have, knowing you're never going to judge me. Like with my family. I don't have to spend my time defending them. You just laugh and accept them. No questions. You have no idea what a relief it is for me."

He knew what she meant. With Cara, it was welcoming not to have to measure every word or watch his back. It had been a long time since Devin had been able to let down his guard and truly be himself. "I think I have a good idea."

She stood up and walked toward him. The morning sun sparkled in her eyes. Devin hated the way he felt at that moment. All he could think about was pulling her into his arms and holding her until she smiled. The thought of having her in his arms warmed his heart and spread outwards. But this wasn't seventeen years ago when he had had the freedom to act on his impulses with Cara.

He cleared his throat in an effort to clear his thoughts. "We'd better see if Roger made it yet."

Cara leaned over the railing of the tower and looked down at the ground below. Devin followed her to the rail and did the same. Below, they found Roger propped up against a lone tree surrounded by a shiny patch of green. His legs were crossed at the ankles and his hands were clasped behind his neck, buried in the shiny green vines crawling up the tree. The smile on his face was almost heartbreaking.

Cara's hands flew to her mouth. Her mouth was agape. "Roger!" she called down.

Roger opened his eyes and waved up at them.

"What are you doing?"

"Just enjoying the morning sun," he called back.

He looked so content and Cara so shocked that Devin didn't know whether to laugh or feel bad for the guy. He was obviously clueless about his current position.

Or he was an idiot.

"But...you're sitting in poison ivy!"

Chapter Four

"Wasn't this guy ever a boy scout?" Devin said as they took the steps down the tower two at a time. "Poison Ivy was taught somewhere between tent pitching 101 and how to dig a hole."

"Ssh. Keep your voice down." Of course, there was more than an ounce of truth in his statement, Cara thought. Roger was born and raised a city boy. Yes, he was cultured in many ways. He knew all the best restaurants to eat at, the best stores to shop, the best *value* of anything around. But a nature lover he wasn't and this disaster just proved it.

Devin stopped at the plywood door at the bottom of the tower and swung around to face her. "No one in their right mind would take a nap in a patch of poison ivy."

Glaring at him, she said, "Who said Roger was in his right mind? He's staying at my mother's house, isn't he?"

"You're too hard on your mother. She only wants the best for you."

"Then she could let me have my life." Cara pushed past him, slamming the makeshift plywood door shut with more force than necessary. The sun and the August heat hit her face with striking force and she had to shield her eyes with the width of her fingers to focus on Roger.

He was now standing, still surrounded by the patches of vines stretching out around the area where he'd been sitting. She groaned, watching him rub his hands on his shorts, then up his arms.

"Are you sure this is poisonous?" he asked, coming toward them.

Devin backed up a few steps. She had to admit she had the urge to do the same, but thought better of it. He might be inept in nature, but he wasn't a leper. At least, as long as he didn't touch her.

"Yes, and don't rub anymore. You're sweating and all your pores are open from running. You're only going to get any oil that's on you into your system faster."

"We'd better get back to the house," Devin suggested. "You're going to need to change and treat your skin."

"The sooner, the better." Roger started to scratch his neck, most probably from nerves than irritation, since she knew he couldn't be reacting to the poison ivy that quickly.

They jogged along the causeway and the road until they made it to the stretch of beach connecting a long line of cottages that led to Cara's parents' house. The familiar scent of seaweed baking in the sun and the cry of seagulls always urged her on.

Cara noticed Roger lagging behind them, clutching his side. They managed to make it all the way to Devin's cottage before they stopped.

"Do you want to rest?" she said, jogging in place.

"Yeah...that sounds...like a good idea," Roger said, winded.

Devin stopped running and blew out a few deep breaths. "Looks like you've got a side-stitch, Roger. Maybe you should walk the rest of the way to work it out?"

"No, no. Just give me a few minutes and I'll be tip-top." Roger plopped onto the sand and bent his body forward.

"It's not that far to my car. I could drive you."

He shook his head again.

"Okay, take a load off," Devin said, walking down toward the shoreline.

To keep her muscles from tightening, Cara walked in paces and moved her arms back and forth. She should have known better than to think Roger could handle a long run his first time out. Although she had to give him credit for the way he'd kept up so far, she should have insisted he stay behind.

While she wasn't use to working out this early in the morning, she had been jogging for many years. She'd always liked working out before going to the office and meeting with clients. Most of her clients preferred afternoon and evening hours, so it wasn't uncommon for her working day to start somewhere around eleven and end around eight at night. Since she wasn't a morning person, it had been a convenience.

To look at Roger, no one would ever call him out of shape. He regularly worked out at the gym where they'd met. She'd only gone to that gym when the owner asked her to remodel the lounge and had given her a temporary membership to get the feel of the place. She'd met Roger during that time and quit going to the gym soon after the remodeling project was complete.

Devin stood by the edge of the tide with his hands propped on his hips, looking out at the ocean. A strange feeling arose in her, pulling her to him. His dark hair was slick with perspiration as were his muscled arms and thighs. His tank top clung to him, leaving nothing for the imagination. She wondered what it would feel like to run her flat palms over the ridges of his back, and press her cheek against his rock-hard chest.

She shook her head to break the thought, wondering where it had come from. Sighing, she walked toward the water's edge as if she were pulled by some invisible magnet. Devin turned to look at her as she drew closer.

"Beautiful, isn't it?" she said.

"I've forgotten just how much," he said, almost in a whisper. Devin turned his sights back to the incoming tide. "How's he doing?"

"Roger's not much on endurance."

"You sound like you're talking from experience. Is everything okay? You know, with the-"

She stuck out her chin, making sure to keep her voice low as she spoke. "I know exactly what you're referring to and you know that's not how I meant it."

He raised his eyebrows. "Everything okay?"

"It's..."

"Fine?"

"Yes, it's...oh, never mind."

A low rumbling chuckle escaped him. "I'd shoot myself if a woman ever said it like that about me."

"I doubt anyone ever has." Cara thought she had said it under her breath, but when he turned to her and gave her a slow smile, one that almost caused her to lose her equilibrium, she knew she'd been caught. She touched her neck, feeling the heat of a blush spread up her cheeks.

A dog barked in the distance—it was more of a whine—and Devin snapped his head up. She turned and looked behind them to find a dog on the edge of the beach. She'd seen the dog before on several occasions and approached him, only to have him run away frightened. It was clear by the way the dog was hobbling that he was injured.

Roger pulled himself up from the sand and they all headed toward the dog. As they approached, the dog crouched down and peered up at them. He was panting heavily, favoring his back paw. The poor thing looked as if he had been put through the ringer and hung out to bake in the hot sun.

As they eased themselves closer, the dog cowered away. But he was clearly in no condition to run like he had before. Devin crouched down on the ground and held out his hand, coaxing the animal toward him. "Come here, boy," he whispered. The deep timbre of his voice was lulling as he continued to inch his way forward. Eventually, he was able to win the animal's trust.

Cara edged closer, but Roger caught her arms and held her back. "What are you doing?" she asked.

"Stay away from it. For God's sake, it might be rabid." Roger's expression was one of disgust.

She pulled her arm out of his grasp. "He's not acting crazy. He's hurt."

"He is a little mangy and his fur is matted on the side." Devin's voice was low and soothing as touched the dog's fur. In turn, the dog seemed to know he had nothing to fear with Devin. "It looks like there might be dried blood on his coat."

Cara's heart dropped. "Do you think he was hit by a car?"

Devin took his attention away from the dog for the first time and looked back at her. "Maybe."

"I thought most towns had leash laws," Roger commented, looking around as if he were looking for a possible owner.

"He might be a stray." Devin gently applied pressure to the dog's back and worked his way down to the back paw's. When he reached the injured leg, the animal yelped. Cara saw Devin flinch as well, as though it pained him to cause any further suffering.

"Not for nothing, Cara, but if this is a stray, we should probably call the animal rescue league. It's their problem, not ours."

With her emotions on edge, she glared at Roger. Yes, he was a very practical person, but she couldn't believe he'd be so heartless as to pass off an injured animal without having any feelings. This was a side of him she'd never seen before. Maybe she had and had chosen to ignore it all this time. It had her wondering how much of Roger she'd ignored in the time they'd been together.

Roger's expression softened, as if he could read her thoughts. "I know you feel bad, but we should leave it to the professionals to handle. It's not our problem."

Devin looked up at them. His jaw was tight and his face drawn. "That may be true, but I'm making it mine."

Careful wrapping his arms under the dog's chest and hind leg, he scooped up the dog, taking care not to injure the other leg any further.

Cara's breath caught in her throat when the dog began to whine. "I can drive you to the veterinarian, if you want."

Devin took each pain-staking step in the stand as if he were holding a bomb about to explode. "No, that's okay. I'll take care of him. You've got Roger to take care of."

An hour later, Roger was waist deep in an oatmeal bath and Cara sat in a wicker chair on the back porch reading the morning paper. As much as she tried, she still couldn't keep her mind off the dog. She'd read the same page three times and still had no idea what the article was about.

Giving in to defeat, she tossed the paper on the table in frustration. Who was she kidding? It wasn't just the dog, it was the love and care Devin had taken in looking after it that she couldn't forget.

As she stood, the back of her thighs clung to the white wicker seat. Everything was hot and sticky, and the moisture filled air was heavy, making it hard to breath. She ran her fingers down her skin, cursing the breezeless heatwave baking the coast. Maybe she'd take a swim to cool off.

As she walked to the kitchen to fetch a refill of lemonade, she twisted her unruly hair into a pony tail at the top of her head.

This is useless, she thought, pulling at the refrigerator door. After all this time, how could she be doubting her relationship with Roger? Devin had been in town no more than twenty-four hours and already she felt her life was in a tailspin.

But of course, that's exactly what her mother wanted. She was sure Ruthie had engineered this whole thing with Devin as a way to drive her and Roger apart. No, her mother was not a bad-hearted woman. Quite the contrary. But her name was firmly placed next to meddlesome and doting in the dictionary. She only wished her mother's obsessive need to throw her and Devin together would end, too.

After pouring a fresh glass of lemonade, Cara placed the pitcher back in the refrigerator, lingering a second or two longer to let the cool air from the fridge bathe her hot skin. She noticed the light of the answering machine on the counter was blinking as she shut the door. Absentmindedly she pushed the button and listened to the response after the beep.

"Ruthie? It's me, Penny Brunelle. I hope I've caught you before you ran out the door. I'm going to be a little late for our appointment, but I can still meet you at my shop. If you have a chance, check with Manny to see if he's free to perform the ceremony. I've cleared it with Father Walker and he agreed it was a nice idea to keep it all in the family. See you at ten."

Cara drummed the counter with her fingers as the beep indicating the end of the message sounded. This was all too strange. Devin was back in Westport. Now Manny was coming home to perform a ceremony? What ceremony? And why was her mother meeting with a wedding consultant?

Devin stood in the examining room of the animal hospital, patting his canine friend in an attempt to keep him calm. He was glad the vet wasn't busy and was able to see him on such short notice. They'd just taken x-rays and he was waiting for the veterinarian to come and give him the results.

The door opened and a salt and pepper-haired woman in a white lab coat walked into the small examination room, holding an x-ray file in her hand. "Mr. Michaels, I'm Dr. Schroeder." She clipped the x-ray to the panel on the wall and switched the light on.

"How bad is he?" Devin asked, looking at the screen, not really sure what he was looking for.

She exhaled. "As we suspected with the initial examination, there was a break in his hind leg and a slight fracture to his pelvis. This type of injury is typical with being hit by a car."

Devin cursed under his breath. His gut reaction was that someone just left the dog to die. Then realizing the company he was in, he gave an apologetic look. "He might have run away before anyone could help him."

"Unfortunately, that happens a lot. He's actually very lucky. His injury isn't life-threatening, but does require some care. The bone is already starting to heal, but unless it is set correctly, the dog won't walk properly."

She flicked off the light on the panel and stood by the table. Leaning over, she felt the injured paw, much to the dog's protest. .

"You mentioned the dog is a stray."

"I think so. We found him on the beach."

"From the condition of his fur and his weight, I'd say you're right." She reached out and began stroking the dog's fur. "He's very lucky you found him. Being dehydrated, he wouldn't have lasted very much longer."

"What will happen to him now?"

She took a deep breath and gave a little shrug. "That depends on you. Treatment can be costly, and he is a stray. If you're willing to take on the responsibility, we can reset his leg, clean him up a little and release him to you in a day or two." Her face was grim, as though she didn't expect him to agree.

Devin stroked the dog behind the ears. "And if I don't take him?"

"Then it's our responsibility to decide at that point." She didn't elaborate beyond that, but he got the vague feeling it meant the future for his new canine friend was grim.

As much as he hated to admit it, a few days ago he would have been more than willing to cut off any emotional connection with the situation. That's what he'd come to.

He sighed, a burning sensation squeezing his gut. That was the whole problem. Somewhere lost in the depositions and court wins and the Manhattan skyline, he'd lost his heart for simple kindness. He thought about the letter still burning a hole in his briefcase from Wendall Palmer, a man accused of murder, swearing his innocence, and reaching out for his help. Could he keep turning his back on that, too?

"I guess I should think of a name for you, huh, buddy?" he said, reaching down and stroking the fur.

Dr. Schroeder straightened her spine. Her smile was wide, as though she were surprised at his decision and obviously happy with the outcome.

So was the dog.

"Who's getting married?" Cara asked, wasting no time getting to the heart of the matter as her mother walked through the kitchen door.

Ruthie cleared her throat and placed the brown paper grocery bag she'd been holding on the counter before answering. She made no eye contact. "Why do you ask, dear?"

Cara crossed her arms across her chest and cocked her head to one side. "You're being awfully secretive. Why didn't you tell me Manny was coming home?"

Ruthie perked up. "Oh, did he call?"

"No, but Penny Brunelle did. She wanted to let you know she'd be late for your *meeting*."

"Oh." Ruthie pulled a double roll of paper towels and frozen orange juice out of the bag and set them on the table.

Cara rounded the table. "That's it? You're not going to elaborate any further?"

"No."

"What's going on, Ma?"

Ruthie waved her hand, making a tsking sound. "So full of questions."

"I wish you were full of answers. Why were you meeting with Penny? And don't tell me that it's because you wanted to invite her to my birthday party because I won't buy it. I haven't seen her since High School."

"You hadn't seen Devin Michaels since just after graduation and look how pleased you were to see him."

"Devin's not a wedding consultant. He's a lawyer. And I'm not talking about him. Now are you going to tell me why you had a meeting with a wedding consultant this morning?"

The screen door slammed as Elsie waltzed into the room. From the look on her face, she was none too pleased. Cara had to wonder if her little fishing expedition was cut short by a little tiff with Albert.

"Who needs a lawyer?" Elsie asked, still weighted down with her fishing gear.

"No one needs a lawyer, Mother," Ruthie said, taking the empty pail from Elsie. Guilt stabbed at Cara when she saw the worried look on her mother's face. *If only she knew the truth...*

Elsie grunted. "Good, they're all shysters. Every last one of them."

"Oh, I think you're being a bit harsh. Devin isn't a shyster."

"Who's Devin?" Elsie stripped off her fishing vest and dropped her pole by broom closet.

"You look a little hot, Grandma," Cara said, taking her by the elbow and leading her to a chair. "Let me get you a glass of lemonade."

"Thanks, Dear, but I need something a little stronger than lemonade."

The lines on Ruthie's face deepened. Apparently Elsie noticed and decided not to push any buttons. "A glass of lemonade will be fine."

Cara cracked a few pieces of ice from the ice tray and plopped them into a glass before adding lemonade. She handed it to Elsie and joined the two older women at the kitchen table.

"You remember Devin," Ruthie said, her expression still drawn with worry. "He was the young man who had dinner with us last night."

"Oh, yes. What a nice man."

Ruthie's smile was hopeful. "He's a lawyer."

Elsie grunted again. "They're all shysters."

Albert must be a lawyer, Cara decided.

She watched as Ruthie wilted. Knowing the act her grandmother was putting on, she couldn't help but feel bad that her mother was being deceived this way. But she had made a promise to her grandmother to keep quiet about her secret affair, and she was going to keep her word.

After a lingering moment of silence, Elsie announced, "I'm going to go scrub this fishy smell off my body. Where's Harold?"

"The hardware store," Ruthie and Cara replied in unison.

"Well, when he gets back, tell him I need him to fix my fishing pole. I had a little...mishap with a shark."

"Have a nice bath, Grandma."

Elsie trudged down the hall toward the staircase. When she was out of earshot, Ruthie whispered. "Do you see what I mean?"

Feigning ignorance, Cara replied, "See what?"

Ruthie cocked her head to one side and shot her a look. "Is this the kind of behavior you would expect from a seventy-eight year old grandmother?"

Cara sucked in her cheeks. "Exactly."

She stifled her mother's retort and got back to the real issue at hand. "Why did you have a meeting with a wedding consultant this morning?"

She wasn't disappointed when Ruthie followed her lead.

Ruthie shrugged. "It's nothing really. Your father and I have decided to renew our wedding vows."

Cara's jaw hit the floor and her heart melted at the thought of her parents standing at the alter renewing their wedding vows after all their married years together. "Really? That's so romantics! That's so...unlike Daddy."

"I know," Ruthie said, almost in a grunt.

Cara chuckled. "Wait a minute. Knowing how you work, I'll bet he doesn't even know about this yet."

Ruthie picked up a dishtowel and swung around, a devilish smile played on her face. "He knows he'll be paying for a wedding."

Cara threw her a suspicious look and proceeded to unload the remaining groceries from the last bag.

"Oh, all right, I told him it was for you."

"Ma!"

"Before you go off on a tizzy, let me explain."

Cara sank down on a kitchen chair, her head still spinning from her mother's revelation. Although this sort of thing shouldn't come as a surprise, she couldn't believe her mother had planned a wedding for her.

Ruthie filled the tea kettle and set it on the burner.

"If I'd told your father that I was planning a ceremony for us, he wouldn't have agreed to it. You know how much your father and I love each other, but let's face it, he's not the sort of man who renews his wedding vows. Baseball is and always was his first priority in life."

"That's not true. Daddy would do anything for you."

"Yes, he would. As long as it wasn't during the ballgame. How many times have I told you the story about how we had to wait to go to the hospital when I was in labor with you because the Sox were playing the Yankees? You're father would never miss that game."

Okay, she was with her mother so far. Romance was not anywhere on the list of her father's priorities in life. Baseball, however, was sitting at the top.

"And he bought that?" Cara asked skeptically.

"Of course he did. I told him you were getting married and he was as thrilled as I was."

"Wait, you've never been happy about the prospect of me marrying Roger. Daddy actually believed you were happy?"

Ruthie made a face, giving Cara cause to believe there was much more to this story than her mother was willing to give up. "He wants to see some grandchildren as much as I do."

"So tell me, how do you propose to tell Daddy this ceremony is really for the two of you?"

"Never you mind. I'll take care of everything. Just don't breathe a word of this to anyone until the ceremony."

Cara actually found herself laughing. Her parents had such a strange relationship. For a minute she wondered if they'd always been like this. But then she remembered the stories her mother had told her about her career and giving it up when she had been born. Had her parents naturally grown into this strange relationship out of boredom? She knew her parents loved each other, but she also knew that her mother had been as career-driven in her youth as Cara had always been. She knew her mother had given it all up for them.

On the other hand, Cara had given up the notion of family for a career. Her relationship with Roger had never threatened her goals because he was as driven as she'd always been. They had an unspoken understanding that theirs was a companionship that was convenient, not meant to clash with the demands of work.

But now her goals were changing, like everything else around her. Manny had left home long ago. Now her parents were leaving, too. And she wanted a family of her own, more than just the occasional convenient *coupling* she had with Roger.

Cara's heart leaped to her throat when she heard a scream reverberate through the house. She and Ruthie ran toward the staircase, hearing the scuffle of feet, the sloshing of water and the slamming of the bathroom door.

"What happened?" Ruthie called up.

Elsie stood at the top of the staircase wearing a terry robe and a scowl on her face. Her fists were firmly planted on her hips.

Cara's hand flew to her mouth. "Oh, my God, I forgot."

Ruthie, still looking daze and bewildered, floated her gaze back and forth from Cara to Elsie.

She bit her bottom lip. "Roger is taking an oatmeal bath."

Cara shouldn't have been surprised when an hour later, Roger was out of the bath and settled into her father's den engrossed in the pile of paperwork. In the eighteen months she'd known Roger, she hadn't one seen him take a day off, or a moment's rest. Facts and figures were his life, not emotions. She'd always found his drive appealing. If he was busy with his own career, he couldn't make demands on her or have expectations that clashed with her own goals.

The unbidden image of her grandmother and Albert on the beach came to mind and she sighed. Just once, she'd like Roger to keep his facts and figures stuffed in his briefcase and take her with that kind of passion.

With thoughts of passion came images of Devin running along the sand, his hair slicked back, every muscle moving in magnificent form. Inside, her body stirred in a way she couldn't control. She'd had this feeling before, but never with Roger.

She walked out into a steam bath outside, hearing the screen door slam behind her. August was living up to being the most humid and hot month of the year.

As she walked on the beach, she pulled off her white canvas sneakers and dug her toes into the warm sand. There were scattered blankets spread across the sand by some of the neighbors and local residents, but being a private beach, it wasn't crowded.

She walked along the edge of the beach and noticed a flock of seagulls picking at the remains of someone's lunch. As she drew closer, all but an ornery bird stayed and picked at the debris until she was close enough to touch it. She picked up the old brown paper bag, discarding it in a garbage can a few yards away. If only people would clean up after themselves and remember that people lived here. This was her home, after all.

She swung around and looked at the beach. The beautiful seascape she'd taken for granted in her teens, the one she'd come to love as an adult, wasn't her home any more. She lived in Boston now in a brownstone building without so much as a porch. And her parents had decided it was their time to leave the home she loved and move on. She couldn't blame them for that. It was their choice.

Cara had left the house not knowing where she was headed. As Devin's cottage came into view, she knew that she'd been unconsciously seeking him out all along.

The cottage was the same one his family had stayed at when they had visited that summer. It was a small, single story house painted an antique ivory with slate-blue trim. It was complete with white picket fence and perennial garden that boasted Indian blanket flowers, hostas and purple coneflower. Even though the cottage was rented out most of the summer, the owners were adamant about the grounds being kept up for the few weeks they stayed there themselves. The sweet scent of the flowers propelled her forward. As she got closer, she saw two hummingbirds dancing on air from one coral flower to the next. When she reached the gate, they flitted away.

Cara pushed through the gate and heard the hinges clank closed behind her. With a few strides up the brick path, she stood at the front door. What was she doing here? she thought as she rapped lightly on the glass. She peeked through the lace curtain hanging on the other side of the door, but could see nothing.

Impatience had her walking around the house when Devin didn't answer the door. A lone car was sitting in the driveway, so he couldn't still at the veterinarian office.

She wasn't prepared for what she found when she rounded the corner.

Chapter Five

Cara found Devin spread out on a canvas hammock, wearing nothing but a pair of faded denim cutoffs. She'd forgotten how the dusting of dark hair on his chest formed into a V and trailed down his flat stomach until it disappeared into his blue jeans. It wasn't like her to stare. But she couldn't tear her eyes away from him.

Every exposed muscle was firm, from his head right down to his toes. His hair was slicked back and wet, as if he'd just taken a shower or gone for a swim.

Her breath caught in her throat, but she forced her greeting past the lump lodged there. "Here you are." Her voice was much too breathless to her own ears. She silently prayed her actions wouldn't betray her thoughts.

"I'm surprised to see you here," he said, pulling himself up from his reclined position on the hammock and dropping his bare feet to the floorboards.

A hot gust of wind blew in from the ocean and tousled his hair about, making him look incredibly adorable, causing her insides to shake like a rickety bridge carrying a runaway train. She'd never reacted to him this way before. She had no idea why she had this strange reaction now.

Lord, had she ever made a big mistake in coming here this afternoon.

"Things got a little crazy this morning with the dog and Roger."

Devin nodded.

She looked around the porch and the immediate perimeter, rubbing her sweaty palms together. Anything to keep from staring at Devin. A pair of leather sandals lay tossed in a heap on the floor with a copper tee-shirt. A stack of newspapers were stacked neatly beside them, looking as if they were still unread.

Cara just stood there, trying to keep her breathing steady, trying not to make a complete and utter fool of herself over what her mind kept straying to. And Devin just stared back at her, at her lips, her eyes...her body, with a hot hunger look in his eyes. There was nothing overt about the way he was staring at her, but it definitely was not the way she was used to him looking at her.

Say something, anything!

"How'd things go at the vet?"

Brilliant.

Devin drew in a short breath that seemed to break the spell between them.

"Better than I expected," he said. "He had a broken leg and a fractured pelvis, but nothing that can't be fixed. I'll be able to pick him up in a day or two."

"You're keeping him?" Apparently, her face registered more than just a little surprise. His low rumbling chuckle sounded like thunder rolling across the sky. She cursed herself for the lightheaded feeling it caused.

Still grinning, he said, "My having a dog shocks you?"

"No," she lied. The past twenty-four hours had been one big shock. If she let herself dwell on any one thing, she'd go nuts. She desperately tried to sound unaffected. "I just can't imagine what you'll do with a dog in Manhattan. And with your schedule..."

"I know a lot of people with dogs in the city. As for my schedule, I can make time when it's important. I'm here, aren't I?"

Heat crept up her already warm skin and she knew she was blushing.

"You'd be wonderful with a dog. I saw the way you handled him this morning. I just can't imagine the dog cooped up in a penthouse apartment."

He grimaced. "I sold the penthouse."

"You did?"

He nodded. "As of right now, this little seaside cottage is my address. That is until I find a new place."

She dropped down to sit on the stairs. Beneath her thigh she felt the splintered treads and carefully shifted herself to look at him.

"So you were serious about leaving Manhattan?"

"Maybe," he said, picking up an empty beer bottle from the railing and motioning to her. "Have one?"

"Sure," she replied.

The screen door slammed behind him as he disappeared into the cottage for a moment. When he came back, he had two open bottles of beer and a glass. He handed the glass and one of the bottles to her.

Cara couldn't help but smile. "You know, I used to chug down from the bottle with you. Since when do you offer me a glass?"

Although her comment was meant as a joke, she noticed his expression was serious. "Like you said, a lot of things have changed since then."

Her smile faded. "You're right. But I have the feeling you're not talking about drinking beer from the bottle."

He sank down to the treads and rested his elbows on his knees, holding the beer bottle in his hand and staring out at the ocean. "No, I'm not."

"What's eating at you?"

"Nothing a good beer buzz won't take care of."

She nudged him in the knee. Bad move, she thought as a jolt of electricity singe her skin where their bodies met. Her awareness of him startled her. It was unlike anything she'd every felt with him before, almost animal. She wondered if he felt it, too.

She looked at his face, into his dark eyes and knew he did, too.

"Where's your other half?" he asked, still not looking at her.

"My other...oh, you mean Roger."

He nodded.

She didn't know why, but the mention of Roger suddenly felt like an intrusion. She certainly never considered him the other half of her. She'd seriously forgotten that he was back at the house working in her father's den. He'd probably be there for the better part of the day.

"He's working. It's not often you can drag Roger away from his desk, so it'll be a working vacation for him."

"All work, no play-" he started the familiar phrase, but Cara finished it.

"Makes Cara go insane."

"Guilty as charged," she said, grinning.

He laughed again in a way that made her want to laugh too, but deep down, there was nothing to laugh about. She'd intended to take these few weeks off for a vacation that a year ago, she'd have fought herself. Now she was getting perturbed with the regimen she'd followed.

"Don't tell me you planned on this being a working vacation." When he gazed at her, it was if he could see right through to the hidden inside. She felt a warm heat that had nothing to do with the mid-August sun, spread through her from her neck to the tips of her toes.

"I planned on a lot of things that don't seem to be going the way I'd hoped. I have always been so certain about everything I wanted." Until now. So much of what she always thought was written in stone was now being wiped clean and re-written. She was changing, people she loved were leaving. At least she could count on Roger to be the same old Roger.

"It was one of the common threads between us."

She couldn't help but smile at that. "Hmmm, and I never made any apologies for it."

"There's nothing wrong with knowing what you want and going after it."

It was his voice. That's what was turning her mind to mush. Its deep timbre sounded so soothing, lulling juxtaposed with the roar of the waves crashing into the shore. If she let herself think about it, she could recall a hundred times they had sat and talked, when she unknowingly sat and listened to the sound of Devin Michaels' voice.

She wondered if it was one of the assets he used in court to win his cases. Probably. She'd seen coverage on CNN of a high profile case he had tried a few years ago. He had been dynamic in the court room. Like he was now, just sitting there, talking with her.

Yes, things were changing all around her, but there was one thing she knew she could count on. Devin Michaels. Deep down, despite the deepening lines on their faces and the distance they'd put between them, she still found it so easy to talk to Devin. It was as if living half their lives apart had had no effect on their friendship.

She watched a woman with a small child of about two walking along the water's edge. The wind blew the crisp white sun cap off the toddler's head and to the sand a few yards up the beach. Mother and child playfully ran after it, hand in hand, giggling. Cara couldn't help but giggle, too. That was the paramount thing that had changed with her, she realized. The most colossal change a person could make in their life was starting a family.

"You really want a baby, don't you?" Devin said quietly as he watched her. He had noticed, even this morning during their run, how Cara reacted every time she saw a child. Who'd have thought that she would ever succumb to maternal urges? She'd never once spoken of motherhood for herself.

But then again, who was he to be surprised? No one would ever believe the changes he'd been thinking about for his own life. He could only imagine how the brass back in Manhattan would react if he decided to actually go through with any of those plans.

Cara was still looking out at the ocean, an expression of longing on her face that he'd never seen before. Her vulnerability overwhelmed him and made him want to touch her. Reaching out, he stroked her cheek with the back of his fingers and gently brushed a wayward strand of hair aside.

She closed her eyes for a mere second, and leaned into his touch. The scent of jasmine drifting to him with the light breeze. She smelled sweet like powder and lemons, as if she'd just made some homemade lemonade before she came over. He heard her moan softly before her eyes flew open.

She stood up quickly, pulling the cuffed edges of her white shorts from her thighs before taking the few steps down the stairs. She brushed her hand along her derriere as if she were suddenly self-conscious. What he wouldn't do to have his hand there, doing that very same thing. He couldn't help but take pleasure in the gentle sway of her hips as she moved. He'd touched her countless times in harmless ways, but never in the way his mind kept insisting he venture now.

And it was an incredibly odd place to go. This was Cara, the girl he use to help climb out of her second floor bedroom window in the middle of the night so they could have a bonfire on the beach and drink cheap liquor. She was the one who played hooky from her summer job just to drive all the way to New Hampshire to buy an old beat-up Firebird he'd been wanting to restore.

And she was the one who listened to countless hours of his hopes for the future, his fears of failure and his devastation when he had learned his father was going to die.

She'd been there, always. No matter what time of day or night. And like that old Firebird, he'd left her and their friendship behind. Looking back, he couldn't understand why. When had their friendship ceased to be important enough that he had no longer needed her?

She twisted around and smiled at him. It was a slow, coy smile that he wasn't use to seeing on her. She'd always been confident. But now, she looked exposed, as if that hot fire that sparked to life, making him want to pull her into his arms, was somehow affecting her, too. And the idea of that wasn't half bad.

"I should be going," she said finally.

He felt his expression collapse. "You just got here."

She was uncomfortable. He could see it by the way she flitted her gaze to him and then away. God, he hated that. That wasn't the way it was supposed to be with them.

"I'm going to see if I can drag Roger away from Dad's den for a little while. There's no telling what my mother is up to now that Roger is staying under the same roof."

"That bad?"

"Actually, no. I have to admit I thought it would be worse than it is. They're trying to stay out of each other's way, which is a blessing. But still..."

Her voice was soft and when a soft sigh escaped her lips he had the incredible urge to touch her mouth, kiss her. Sure, he'd kissed her before. But as a friend. Not at all the way he wanted to take her now.

Disappointment hit him straight in the chest. He didn't want her to leave. He wanted to sit there—all day if he could—and just look at her, talk to her. It had been a long time since he'd felt this much at peace being with another person, not worrying about weighing his words or thoughts. It was what he had always loved most about him and Cara.

He pulled himself up from the stairs. "Let me get a shirt. I'll walk you back."

She shook her head and nibbled on her bottom lip. "That's okay. I could use some time alone. It's a little crowded back home."

He watched her pull her sneakers off her feet and step into the wet sand. What the hell was he thinking? After two days with Cara, did he really think he could figure out how the last seventeen years had affected her?

No, he had his own life plan to figure out. Starting with whether or not he was going to take the Palmer case. That pile of newspaper clippings and court documents weren't going to get read watching Cara's hip sway as she walked along the surf.

But he couldn't help himself. He watched her anyway because it felt good. He kept his eyes on her even as he heard the sound of the phone ringing in the house, until she was completely out of sight. When the ringing persisted, he took the stairs two at a time and bolted through the back door to catch the caller.

He said, "Hello," just as the screen door slammed behind him.

"I'm glad you're in, Devin. I was just about to hang up." Ruthie's voice was as pleasant as ever. "I was wondering if you could do me a bit of a favor."

He slumped into a kitchen chair. "You know I can never refuse you, Ruthie."

"That's what I'm counting on."

Devin chuckled. She was up to something all right and he'd be damned if he wasn't going to find out what it was. "What can I do for you?"

"Well, it seems I've gotten myself in a pickle." Her tone was serious.

He frowned. Reaching back, nestling the phone between his shoulder and chin, he opened the refrigerator to grab another beer. "Sounds like trouble. Is it a legal issue? Something with the sale of the house?"

Ruthie's charming laughter came flowing over the phone line. "Lord, no. Nothing at all like that."

He breathed a slight sigh of relief. "Good."

"I happened to see Penny Brunelle this morning, and we got to talking, and I mentioned you were in town. Do you remember Penny?"

He thought a minute. "No."

"She graduated with Cara. Very nice girl, has her own bridal boutique. Anyway, she's going through a divorce and with you being a lawyer and all..."

"I'm a defense attorney, Ruthie. I'm not sure I can be of any help. Unless, of course, she tries to kill him."

Ruthie's laugh was rich. "Oh, I know, but maybe you could have dinner with her tonight and put her at ease...about her settlement, of course."

He half grinned. "Of course."

Somehow he knew there was more than just white frosting on a devil's food cake here. Ruthie had been known to bake a few *harmless* schemes in her day where Cara was concerned. But this time, Cara wasn't part of the recipe. She was cooking up something and Devin wondered just what that was.

"So will you come?"

He shrugged, looking at the pile of reading material strewn about the kitchen table, waiting to be read.

Cara said she needed time alone to think. He was positive she could see how hot he got just watching her this afternoon, and it had nothing to do with the temperature being close to one hundred degrees! After the way his thoughts had been pulling him to her, maybe a diversion would help put his mind and his libido back on track, back to the way things use to be with them.

"Sure, why not."

"Great. I took the liberty of making reservations for seven at the *Whaler's Inn*."

He scribbled down directions to Penny's house and the time. He washed down the dregs of his beer and stared at the ink on the notepad. He tore out the directions and added the notepad to the pile on the table. He wasn't going to get any work done on the Palmer case tonight if he was thinking about Cara. Going on a blind date wasn't exactly his style, but Penny Brunelle might just be the distraction he needed.

"Ruthie and a bridal consultant," he mumbled to himself. "I wonder who's getting married?"

Cara re-read the same page from the home interiors magazine she'd been trying to read for the past fifteen minutes. This was becoming a habit. Giving up, she tossed the magazine to the end table and wiped the sweat off her forehead with the back of her hand. This heatwave was just another thing to add to the list of things starting to bug her.

Why had she left Devin's so quickly? She sighed heavily. Because every time he looked at her she wanted to fall into his arms and not let go. She wanted to be with him. But she couldn't stand the feelings she was having for him, so she took the cowards way out and left.

Now she was just plain bored and wished she was back at Devin's cottage with him. She'd already gone into the den twice in the last hour to see if Roger was done working and got the non-committal "almost". She'd be damned if she'd interrupt him again.

It had been a bad idea to invite Roger, she decided as she plopped down on the back stairs, arching her back to pull out the kinks. The sun was sinking in the horizon, giving a milky film to the water and an amber color to the sky. At least there was an occasional breeze to salve the heat and humidity. She only wished she could find something that would salve her own unrest.

The slap of the screen door against the wooden frame jarred her and caused her to turn around. "Hi, Ma," she said, slightly annoyed that it wasn't Roger.

Ruthie blotted the sweat from her neck with a white dishtowel. "Are you still hungry, dear?"

"We just finished dinner an hour ago."

"I know, but I'm in the mood for some fried clams."

A half hour later Cara stood by the takeout window of the *Whaler's Inn*. The smell of fried seafood filled her head immediately. She wasn't hungry, but she needed to get out of the house and stretch. Anything was better than sitting at home brooding.

Stuffing the change the waiter had just given her into her pocket, she clutched the bag of fried clams and turned to leave. As she walked over the pavement, the sound of her white flip-flop sandals slapping the soles of her feet entranced her until she heard a familiar low rumbling laugh.

Her heart pounded in her chest. It could be anyone. But no, she knew the sound of *that* laugh. She plopped the bag of takeout on the hood of her car and spun around, scanning the parking lot to see if it was actually Devin. And then she recognized him, sitting at a table on the back porch of the restaurant. Her heart lifted until she saw the tall, leggy, blond wearing a white mini-dress seated practically in his lap.

Penny Brunelle hadn't changed much. Married three times already since high school, she'd made a career out of arranging weddings for herself as well as others. Now what was she doing with Devin?

Cara bit down on her bottom lip. She didn't want to know.

If you have any sense at all, Cara, you'll get in the car and drive away before they notice you. What business was it of hers that Devin had a date? So he'd come to Westport for her birthday party, but that didn't mean he had to stay in her back pocket the whole time. She clenched her teeth as she watched Penny trying to climb into his.

Although from the several rows of cars that sat between them she couldn't hear a single word they were speaking, Cara suddenly felt like she was eavesdropping on Devin's private conversation with Penny. She did hear all the bells and whistles Penny was clanging to attract Devin's attention.

She watched as Penny stood up, pulling Devin to a stand, and wrapped her arms around his waist, gyrating her hips as she moved. It became a conscious effort for Cara to keep her fingernails from breaking skin on the inside of her palms.

And to breathe. She needed to breathe. Forcing a lung full of air into her chest, she yanked the car door open. They were going to kiss and Cara did not want to be around to see it. She'd already gotten a bigger eyeful than she wanted or needed for one night.

So what if Devin has a date with her high school rival?

So what if Penny was scoping out husband number four?

For all she cared, they could go home and...

Pain brought her thoughts back to the present. Cara glanced down at her hand and realized she'd been digging her car keys into the flesh of her palm. She jammed the keys into the ignition and roared the engine to drown out her thoughts. Almost forgetting the food on the hood, she opened the door, retrieved the bag and slammed the door shut. She turned the corner onto the main road and kicked her foot on the accelerator, drumming her fingers on the steering wheel.

You're acting like an idiot! There was no reason for her to be all hot under the hood about seeing Devin with Penny. Just because she chose to spend the night alone, didn't mean Devin had to stay home and brood, too. He had his own life that didn't include her or their friendship. Penny was an attractive woman and Devin was a big boy. He could date anyone he wished.

Besides, she had Roger.

For the rest of the ride home, she worked on trying to reason why that was a plus.

Chapter Six

The air was still crisp as Cara jogged up the brick path, leading to Devin's cottage. The sun was floating over the water just waiting to burn off the morning dew. The sweet scent of garden phlox and princess roses filled her head as she climbed the porch steps.

This had to be a first. She'd forced herself out of bed after setting her alarm for five a.m., deciding she'd be the one to initiate the morning run.

She was nuts and that was all there was to it, she realized as she jogged in circles on the porch, trying to muster up the courage to knock on the door. She had no idea if Penny had stayed the night, but the idea of interrupting a morning interlude seemed, well, kind of devilish.

It fit her current mood rather well.

She stopped jogging and blew out a cleansing breath before raising her knuckles to the glass door and rapping on the wooden frame. "There just may be a little bit of Mom in me after all," she whispered.

She only had to knock once. Within seconds, she heard the sound of footsteps on the wooden floor, coming closer to the door. Regret gripped her stomach, and she had the fleeting desire to bolt while she still had the chance.

The door flew open and she was greeted by Devin's smoky sleepy-eyed gaze. A flurry of emotions whirled around her. The devilish feelings that filled her just moments ago turned to panic. *Maybe this wasn't such a good idea.*

"You're awake?" Devin said, his voice and expression registering all the shock she felt inside.

His hair was disheveled, as if he'd been raking his fingers through it. He was wearing the now-wrinkled copper colored T-shirt she'd seen balled up on the back porch the day before and the same faded cut-offs. He looked as if he hadn't had a minute of sleep. And he was absolutely gorgeous. She actually hated him for it.

"I'd have to be if I'm standing here."

Devin moved aside so she could gain entrance. "But you said you never get up this early. I had to drag you out of bed yesterday."

My point was to do the same to you, too.

"Look how you've influenced me."

Cara lifted her hands up in the air as if she were parading a new dress. "Got any coffee?"

She wandered down the hallway toward the kitchen. She took a quick glance through the open bedroom door and noticed it was empty. Amazing how a little solitude can do a girl some good. Especially when Devin was the one sleeping alone.

"Yeah, but it's a few hours old. Let me make a new pot."

A twisting pain she refused to call jealousy gripped her gut. She glanced at the bathroom door. Open and empty.

"Up all night?"

"I slept an hour or two, but mostly tossed in bed."

I'll just bet.

"I'll take the dregs of the pot first."

He grimaced and jammed his fingers through his hair. "That's suicidal."

So is dating Penny Brunelle, but Devin would find that out soon enough. Instead she said, "Running at five thirty a.m. can be a bit life-threatening, but you'll have no problem with it."

After pulling a mug from the rack on the wall, Cara emptied the pot, and topped the coffee off with a dab of milk and spoonful of sugar. If the color of the liquid and the bitter taste were any indication, Devin was right about the coffee haing been sitting for hours.

She dumped the disgusting liquid down the drain and quickly helped Devin make a fresh pot. When it was finished brewing she poured them both a cup while Devin cleared the cluttered kitchen table.

He moved a large stack of books, a laptop computer that was still plugged into the phone jack and countless pencils and highlighters that were scattered about.

"I'll just be another second with this," Devin said.

As she pushed aside one of the books, that was about six inches thick, so she could put down her coffee mug, she read the binding. It was marked *The People vs. Wendall Palmer.* "A little light reading while you vacation, huh?" she teased.

"Just some research for a court case."

His lips lifted on one side and her breath hitched in her throat. She turned her attention to the book again to rid herself of the longing she felt while Devin closed up the computer and pulled the cords from the wall. He clear the area in front of her and began stacking all the paraphernalia in a pile on the opposite side of the table.

She gave an exaggerated sigh. "What was it you said to me yesterday about working vacations?"

He gave her a questioning glance, stopping short in his motion for a moment before returning to his task. "This was part of the reason I took time off."

She placed her hand over her chest, feigning dejection. "And all this time I thought you came for my birthday party."

His tired expression lit up. "Speaking of which, what do you want for your birthday?"

"You mean a present? You don't have to get me anything. I'm just happy to see you."

The truth was, she was *too* happy to see him. Being this close to Devin, even seeing him tousled and sleep deprived was messing up her thought process. This wasn't the same as when they were kids. This was different, deeper.

Cara cleared her throat. "But I'm not letting you out of going to the festival with me tonight."

He reached for the last book and brushed passed her, his warm skin grazing her arm. For a split second, he paused in motion and stared at her. His dark eyes grew impossibly wide and soulful, suddenly full of life. It was as if he'd finally woken up with that single point of contact. His arm lingered there where there skin touched, teasing her with its electric current, bringing with it a fire that started deep inside her, growing with every passing second and spreading heat outward. His lips were slightly parted as if in waiting. His gaze dropped to her lips, causing her pulse to pound. Was he going to kiss her?

But he didn't. As if startled himself by his own reaction, he pulled back and sat down opposite her at the kitchen table, pushing his chair and balancing it on the back legs until the back hit the wall.

"Ah, the festival, yes. I still think you cheated yesterday," he said, eyeing her over the rim of his coffee mug. Despite the mug hiding his mouth, she could see the slow smile creeping into his expression. He was teasing her. Or attempting to at any rate. But the heat she'd seen in his eyes a moment ago remained.

He *had been* going to kiss her. She drew in a slow breath of air, somehow vaguely disappointed he'd chosen against it.

She straightened in her chair and took a sip of coffee, waiting until the hot liquid burned its way passed the lump in her throat. "It's the lawyer in you. You don't have any plans for tonight, do you?"

She was treading in murky waters. She waited with bated breath as he paused a minute as if he needed to consult his mental calendar. Had last night been so wonderful with Penny that they'd made plans again?

Damn, men are all alike. They get all hot and bothered about some things and then sucked in by a tight mini-dress and gyrating hips.

"Will it be just you and me, or is Roger going, too?"

She'd mentioned it to Roger and while he wasn't thrilled with the idea of going on "kiddie" rides, as he put it, he did give her his word that he would go. She knew the real reason was to please her after working so much these past few days.

"Actually, he decided to come with us. Is that okay?"

He frowned and her heart sank a notch or two. What was he getting at? Was he afraid of being paired up or was it that he'd hoped to invite Penny? Before he could think to ask otherwise, she blurted out, "I was hoping you'd ride the double Ferris wheel, just like old times."

His smile widened and her heart leaped to her throat. Devin Michaels had a way of making her forget who she was. Or remember who she use to be. She wasn't quite sure which. But when he looked at her like this, all she could think about was the way his smoky eyes devoured her with his gaze.

He dropped his coffee mug on the table and leaned closer. His voice was rich and husky, making her heart sing. "I'm all yours."

Now this was a bright idea. As they walked through the wall-to-wall crowd of people all gather along the wharf in New Bedford where the yearly Portuguese Festival was held, Devin seriously considered leaving. Maybe it was him, but it seemed every person who passed by had the arm of someone else. And what was he doing? He was alone, chasing Cara and Roger's shadow, wishing he was the one taking Cara's hand in his.

He laughed at the irony. Even the thought of having her next to him, just holding her small hand in his, was enough to make his body respond. All he could think about was how he wanted to make this incredible woman, his best friend, become his lover.

He wasn't exactly sure when it had happened, but somewhere over the last twenty-four hours his feelings for Cara had changed.

He should have asked Penny Brunelle if she wanted to come with them. Not that he'd actually wanted to date her again after warding off last night's gropefest. No, he'd seen women of Penny's caliber more times than he cared to remember. But at least if she were here, this sudden sexual urge for Cara that had come out of nowhere wouldn't be taking control of him.

He sighed as they walked through a crowd of people waiting in line to have their faces painted by a make-up artist. Cara turned back, as if to make sure he was still there and she gave him a crooked grin. That smile alone almost made the uncomfortable feeling nagging at him bearable.

"Want to get painted?" Devin mouthed, waggling his eyebrows.

Cara darted a glance to the people in line and giggled. But then her eyes caught sight of something past the crowd and her whole expression changed to wonder.

"Oh, look," she said, sprinting to a display table. Curiosity had him following her, or maybe it was just the bright look in her eyes that reminded him of a child's on Christmas morning.

He was happy enough she wasn't glued to Roger's side at the moment. The thought of Cara with another man, one that she'd been intimately involved with for almost two years, nagged at him. He'd been naked with plenty of women. Beautiful women, he vehemently reminded himself. But the twisting knot that clutched him hard when he was with Cara and Roger wouldn't ease up. It was high time he stopped denying it was jealousy.

"These carousels are beautiful," Cara said to the woman behind the booth.

The woman returned a warm smile, obviously pleased with Cara's appraisal. "They're hand made by a local craftsman."

Cara placed her finger on one of the painted wooden horses lined up on the outside of the wooden stand. With a gentle motion, she pushed it around and around. The ribbons adorning the center pole and strung out to each of the twelve horses wound around the center pole. She let go and the carousel spun as each horse moved up and down with the motion, like a real carousel.

Devin stared at Cara's childlike expression. He couldn't help it. God, she was just too damned beautiful. She wore her long wavy hair down tonight, and the cool ocean breeze lifted her natural curls. He'd always like it when she wore her hair down, giving her a air that was almost untamed. He had the most incredible longing to tangle his fingers in her wild curls.

"Do you remember-" she started to say, but stopped short, glancing sheepishly at him and then the saleswoman as if she'd forgotten anyone else was there with them.

Devin knew exactly what memory had made its way back to her mind. He'd been thinking of the same night.

"Fourth of July at Riverside."

Her face lit up like a blazing star. Of course, all the flashing white and red lights from the carnival displays might have had something to do with that, too. But no, he knew she was deep in the memory of their first and only real kiss. And so was he. It was amazing how vividly he remembered the feel of her soft lips pressed against his. And how much he wanted to relive that memory, see if her lips still were as soft as they looked right now.

They gazed at each other, both transfixed with the memory for a lingering moment.

That is, until Roger broke in.

"I went to Riverside once because my girlfriend at the time wanted to see a soap opera star who was going to be there." He reached up to his neck, which was covered with pink calamine lotion, and began to scratch. "I think it rained."

"How much is it?" Cara asked, pulling her gaze away.

Without looking at the tag, the woman advised, "Three hundred and fifty dollars."

"Let's go," Roger sputtered, tugging on Cara's arm.

Cara's expression faltered slightly. "Thank you," she said to the woman. She dug her hands in the pockets of her cutoff shorts and started walking away from the table with Roger at her side, the light in her eyes fading.

Devin couldn't help but notice the sneer on Roger's face.

Or how much Cara truly loved that carousel.

Devin fell into step with her. "Aren't you going to get it? I know you'd love to have it."

Cara's face was almost regretful. "I didn't bother to bring my checkbook tonight," she said quietly.

He laced his fingers with her, not caring anymore that Roger was there, and tugged her back a step. "Come on. Maybe she'll hold it for you. We can come back later or—"

Roger waved his hand. Although they were out of earshot from the table, he kept his voice low. "The wooden ones aren't worth as much as the porcelain ones. What they're asking for here is highway robbery. It's not worth it."

Worth it to whom? Devin wondered. Where did this guy get off bursting Cara's excitement over a price tag? It wasn't as if any of them were in a position to have to cut coupons and eat nothing but macaroni and cheese.

Glancing at Cara, he saw a trace of embarrassment etched in her expression and decided not to press the issue. He got the distinct impression this wasn't something new to her, just annoying.

"If you really want a carousel, we can get one when we get back to Boston," Roger added, taking her by the hand again.

Anger coiled deep inside Devin and it was all he could do to keep from taking a swing at Roger. Cara couldn't help it if Roger was a jerk, but what had gotten into her? If it were him making those same statements, Cara would think nothing of turning around and telling him where to stuff it. At least the old Cara would. What had this Roger guy done to his Cara? *His Cara?*

"Cara?"

She smiled weakly. "It's just one more thing to bring home to my condo with all the other boxes I've packed. Really, it's okay. There's a shop on Newbury Street that has carousels like this. I can always pick one up there."

Devin pointed through the crowd. "Well, let's at least ride the carousel. You always loved that." With their hands still joined, Devin pulled Cara through the crowd to the ticket line.

"I haven't done anything like this since..."

She looked up as if she were searching the deepest recesses of her mind. Then she looked at Devin, laughing. God, how he missed that fanciful laugh. He had never realized it until just then.

"I think I was with you the last time I rode a carousel."

Roger shook his head. "Look at you two. Don't you get tired of this kind of thing?"

"No," they both said in unison, laughing.

Devin bought enough tickets for a couple of rides and they waited in line until it was their turn. It was no surprise that Roger decided to remain on the sidelines. All this togetherness was beginning to give Devin the hives as bad as Roger's poison ivy. Well, maybe not. Roger was getting pretty red under the collar.

Devin was just seeing red.

They climbed aboard the carousel and Cara chose a pretty white mare wearing a golden bridle with painted roses trailing off the mane. He chose the black stallion just opposite her. All the stars in the sky were drowned out by the flashing lights of the carnival and the zillions of red and white lights ablaze on the carousel ceiling.

Cara reached up and gripped the golden roped pole in front of her as the carousel began to move. The music blared, drowning out the sounds of the crowded wharf. She hadn't felt so much excitement in years. And all it was was a carnival ride!

As the horses moved up and down on the platform, the familiar tune *Let Me Call You Sweetheart* played. It fed the festive mood riding high inside her. The sweet smell of fried dough and cotton candy hung heavy in the humid night.

Unlike the dream she had had the other day, Devin was here beside her instead of standing on the sidelines. She glanced over at Devin and smiled. The wind whipped through his dark hair as if he was riding a real wild stallion. As he reached up to catch the brass ring that teased them with each passing, the blur of the crowd in the perimeter took on a surreal look. All she could focus on was Devin.

If it hadn't been for the fact that she knew Roger wasn't having a good time, she'd be having a fabulous time. That crack shot comment he'd made about the wooden carousel was something she'd become immune to. She'd let it go, rather than make a scene in front of Devin or hurt the saleswoman's feelings.

She saw the look on his face when they'd seen the wooden carousel, and she knew he had seen how much she loved it. When they walked away from the table empty-handed, his face registered pure shock, as if he were disappointed by her cowardice.

With that embarrassing scene behind them now, Cara was starting to relax again. She couldn't remember having so much fun. At least not in recent years. Her face muscles actually hurt from laughing and smiling so much. She knew without a doubt that it was being with Devin that had cut through the melancholy she'd been feeling over her parents move. When she was with him, she didn't feel so alone.

His laughter broke into her thoughts and she was once against transfixed by the magic of the moment.

"Here comes the brass ring," Devin called out to her over the music.

"Try to catch it."

Laughing, he reached one hand up while holding the twisted gold pole in front of him for support. Her eyes fixed on the brass ring speed toward him. When it was almost upon him, he reached for it, but brushed right by his fingertips.

"Missed!" he said, settling back down on the saddle.

Cara had to wonder just what else *she'd* missed as the ride wound down and the revolving motion of the horses finally came to a halt.

Next was the double Ferris wheel, which they decided to ride three times before the cotton candy in Cara's stomach told her it was time to get off. When they walked through the gate at the end of the ride, Cara spotted Roger, who again decided to stay behind.

"Are you finally ready to leave?" he said, more than a little annoyed.

"Already?"

"I'm sorry, but a guy can get kind of lonely standing on the sidelines all night."

Cara's heart sank. Roger was right. Although she was having the time of her life with Devin, it couldn't have been much fun for him.

"I had more fun tonight than I've had in years," Devin said, looking at her with what she thought was regret in his gaze. "It's a shame to have it end now."

With that Devin turned his attention in the opposite direction. Cara used that opportunity to talk to Roger privately.

"You really want to leave?"

Roger sighed. "Look, you know this whole thing isn't my kind of entertainment. If you want to spend some time with Devin, that's okay with me."

"You won't be upset?" She knew better than to think Roger would be jealous.

Roger made a face. "Darling, I like to think of myself as an open guy. I know how you feel about me."

"We all drove together. I don't want you to have to come back and get us."

"Actually, I'm not sure Devin would mind if we both left now."

"What do you mean?"

Cara twisted around and looked in the direction Roger was staring. Devin was turned in the opposite direction, talking to someone. He was standing in front of the person and all Cara could see were long slender fingers with bright red painted nails brushing up and down Devin's arm.

Her stomach recoiled. She would have liked to think that all this person was doing was asking for directions to the port-a-john, but that would be ridiculous. Almost as ridiculous as the jealousy that gripped her when she saw the woman standing in front of Devin was Penny Brunelle.

Yes, this time she new what she was feeling was jealousy. She'd been having a wonderful time having Devin all to herself. She didn't want to think about sharing him.

Taking her by the arm, Roger said, "Maybe it's time for us to go."

"You're leaving?" Devin was standing by Cara's side now, a look of regret etching his features.

It hadn't taken but a moment for Penny to cozy up next to him. She wore a provocative black catsuit with plunging neckline. She was on the scoop for a husband all right. And what better place to advertise than a festival where there were certain to be eligible men.

"Afraid so," Roger said, holding out his hand to shake Devin's.

"I hope you don't mind if I hang around for a while," Devin announced, which brought a fulsome smile from Penny.

A frosty chill filled Cara and she hoped it wasn't evident in her tone. "I don't feel right leaving you. We drove, so how will you get home?"

"That won't be a problem. My car is certainly big enough for the two of us," Penny said in her throaty voice. Cara wondered if it was natural or years of practice with husband number one, two and three.

"Then I guess it's all set then," Cara said quietly.

"I'll see you tomorrow," he said.

"Okay."

It wasn't like Cara to play the coy maiden. But she was jealous. No doubt about it. And she hated the feeling.

She turned and walked away, through the crowd. Just like in her dream, except this time she was with Roger.

Her foul mood hadn't eased up when she and Roger finally reached the car. Jovial voices of the people having fun and the sound of carnival music drifted through the air, letting her know what she was missing.

She looked back at the bright lights staining the night sky and remembered the fun she'd been having with Devin, his lighthearted smile, and his taste for adventure that matched her own.

She sighed, her shoulders sagging.

Roger revved the engine as she got into the front seat next to him, slamming the door.

"Everything okay, Cara?" he asked, reaching over and taking her by the hand. It was a gesture that use to bring her comfort and now held no magic.

She hesitated a moment. Everything was *not* all right. She'd just left Devin at the festival with Penny Brunelle and she was jealous as all get out, regardless of whether or not she had a right to be.

"I'm fine."

As they drove away from the festival, she turned back once and realized she'd just left a piece of herself behind. Maybe that was the demon she'd been fighting all along. This feeling that something was missing, something that only seemed to fade when Devin was near, was her wake up call, a magical fire that brought her to life.

And she'd just left all her magic back at the carnival.

Chapter Seven

"What do you mean you're not going?"

Ruthie stood over Cara as she lay in her bed. Although Cara had pulled the pillow over her head, she was more than certain her mother's hands were propped on her hips and she was scowling.

She whipped the pillow off and sat up straight. "I just don't feel like going down to Penny's shop to try on bridesmaid dresses. You have to admit that having bridesmaids for renewing your wedding vows is a little..." She searched for the right words that wouldn't offend her mother.

"Un-traditional?" Ruthie supplied for her.

Cara shrugged. "Why don't you just pick out the most beautiful dress in the shop and I'll pay for it. I thought I'd stay back here today and help Daddy with some packing. You only have another week before you're moving."

Ruthie groaned and placed the back of her hand on Cara's forehead.

"What are you doing?" Cara asked.

"You must have a high fever if you'd rather stay here and listen to your father scream about missing the Yankees game tonight, instead of going shopping."

Cara plopped her hands down on the bedsheets. "Great. You planned my birthday party for a day the Yankees are playing the Sox? Is Daddy even going to be here tonight?"

"Of course, I had Larry lend him a Watchman. Even if his mind is on the game, he'll be with us in body. Besides, I didn't know about the game when I planned the party. It's not like your father gives me a rundown of their schedule."

Ruthie took both of Cara's hands and began tugging her. "If you don't go down to try on a gown, your father will get suspicious. Remember, he thinks this wedding is for you."

Cara had to laugh. For once it seemed that her mother was working her antics on someone other than her. She had to admit that she'd expected things to be a lot worse on this vacation than they had been so far.

On the other hand, Devin had gone home with Penny Brunelle last night. The last thing she wanted to do was get pinned into a dress and have to listen to every detail of Penny's evening with Devin.

"You're supposed to be my maid of honor. I want everything to be perfect."

Cara chest squeezed at that. It was truly romantic that her parents were renewing their wedding vows after all these years together. Having her brother perform the ceremony would make it all the more special. The least she could do was to rise to the occasion and help her mother with the details.

"I'm not being a very good maid of honor, am I?" Cara said with regret.

Ruthie smiled and gave her a hug. "I couldn't ask for a more perfect person for the job. Now let's get dressed so we're not late."

To Cara's dismay, when they arrived at the shop, it was empty except for Penny. That meant they had Penny's undivided attention. They'd spent the better part of an hour sifting through gowns on the racks before they headed into a large back dressing room with an armful of dresses to try on.

She was happy when her mother took the lead in keeping the conversation going with Penny. Ruthie went into her usual monologue of wanting grandchildren and how she'd never have that particular pleasure in life if she left it up to Cara. Normally, Cara would have been annoyed and fired back with some quick retort about how she was a grown woman who didn't need a man to take out of garbage or add a can of oil to the car.

But she took the small blessing that Ruthie was keeping Penny occupied for the moment. Cara didn't have to hear any details of the previous evening.

The first two dresses Cara tried on were awful. They belonged back on the rack. She stood in front of the full length mirror holding the third dress to her chest and stared at her reflection. The dress was beautiful and she immediately fell in love with it.

She slipped into the dress and stood with her back to her mother. "Button me, will you?"

Ruthie gasped. "Oh, I think this is the one."

When her mother was through, Cara climbed up on the podium, and looked at her reflection. The pale peach gown had a jewel-neckline and delicate lace covering the form-fitting bodice.

Her mother held her hands to her chest, tears glistened in her eyes. "You look simply beautiful, darling."

Cara couldn't help but feel giddy. The dress looked almost magical on her, as if it was made just for her and her alone. "I can't wear this one."

Ruthie wilted. "Why not? You don't like it?"

"Perhaps you'd like something more formal. Because of the tea-length style, a lot of women choose this type of dress for second time around weddings. But it could certainly be worn for a first wedding."

Cara stifled a retort, wondering what Penny was going to wear for her fourth time around.

She spun on the podium in her bare feet and watched as the chiffon skirt lift with the motion. The peach color was a nice contrast to her tanned skin and dark hair and eyes.

Penny smiled with businesslike satisfaction married with her uncanny charm. "It truly is a beautiful wedding dress."

Ruthie coughed.

"Yes, it would be perfect for a simple wedding, except I'm not the one who's getting married. Didn't you tell her what was really going on, Ma?"

"I, ah, yes," Ruthie stammered.

"This is a beautiful dress. But I think it's a bit too showy for a maid of honor."

Cara stepped down from the podium and took her mother's hand, giving it a gentle squeeze.

"It's suppose to be your day. All eyes should be on you, Ma, not me."

"Thank you, dear. But I really do think this is the one. Don't you, Penny?"

"Simply beautiful. Devin will think so, too, I'm sure."

Cara crinkled her eyebrows. "Devin? What does Devin have to do with all this?"

"I thought Devin was the-" Penny began to say before Ruthie cut in.

"Devin is going to be the best man," Ruthie blurted out.

Turning to her mother, Cara felt suspicion raking up her spine. "Why Devin? Why didn't you ask one of Daddy's friends?"

"I can't risk your father finding out until the morning of the ceremony. By then it will be too late for him to back out. He'll have already spent his money. I simply can't risk it."

"I'm not sure that Devin will still be in town on Labor Day."

Knowing how her mother's mind worked, a thought occurred to her. "Why didn't you ask Roger?"

Ruthie's lips thinned. "I had no way of knowing if he'd be able to attend."

Cara's mouth flew open, and she forgot they weren't alone. "Ma, didn't you think I'd be taking him?"

Ruthie huffed. "What am I supposed to think? You've been living under the same roof for a week and you hardly see each other. What does that say?"

A chasm in her mind widened, revealing a glimpse of what her mother was up to a bit more clearly.

"Did you tell Daddy that I was marrying Devin?"

Ruthie lowered her gaze. "I doubt your father would have given his blessing otherwise. You know how fond he's always been of Devin," she said, as if that made perfect sense for her behavior.

"Doesn't he find it a bit *odd* for me to have one man living under our roof and marrying another?"

"The conversation didn't even get that far. You father is just happy to have you married, at this point. You know this time of year that if it isn't connected to baseball, chances are your father isn't paying attention anyway."

Cara stood straight as a board, her fists balled by her side like a two year old about to have a tantrum. She couldn't believe her ears.

"So you just invited Devin and set up this story. First the booties and now you're picking out my husband? You're incredible!"

"You have to admit Devin is a far better choice than Roger. One day you'll see that I'm right and you'll be as happy with Devin as I am with your father." Ruthie tossed her frosted hair back and forth to make her point.

"What are you talking about? I don't have to admit any such thing. I've chosen to be with Roger. You're just going to have to accept that."

Cara gripped the skirt of her dress and stormed into a private dressing room to escape her fury. Much to her amazement, it followed her, and in her two by two stall, she began to wonder just what she was so angry about. She was used to her mother's antics. This latest classic Ruthie trick shouldn't surprise her.

So why was she so angry? Her mother had never hidden the fact that she wanted Cara to marry and give her grandchildren. But it never seemed like a possibility with Roger. She'd always known Roger liked things just the way the were, simple, uncluttered. Safe. Family was something he'd always deemed clutter, which was mainly the reason she never approached him about her sudden change of heart regarding children and family.

She carefully placed the delicate dress back on a hanger and opened the drapes to the dressing room. Only then did she realize that the rest of her clothes were in the larger, open dressing room with full length mirrors. Being humble in your underwear was hard, but at least she was only with her mother. She only hoped catsuit Penny was long gone and on to other things by now.

Devin tried his best to keep the shock from creeping into his tone, but the look on Cara's face was truly hilarious and he just had to laugh. It was a deep belly laugh that did wonders to lift his mood. "Who's getting married?"

"This isn't funny, Dev. She's doing it to me, again."

Cara plopped down on the back stairs of Devin's cottage and rested her elbows on her knees.

"I'm almost thirty-five years old and she still treats me like I'm a teenager."

He coughed the rest of his laughter out of his system before joining Cara on the stairs. Trying his best to keep from laughing at the absurdity of the situation, he began in a more serious tone, "Maybe that's because you still treat her like your mother."

Her eyebrows furrowed, and she looked at him like he had five heads. "What the hell is that suppose to mean? She *is* my mother!"

"Yeah, and you're still knocking heads with her just to goad her." He shrugged. "Why don't you see it from her point of view?"

Her face registered mock panic. "You're nuts if you are seriously starting to see the crazy logic in her thinking."

He chuckled. "I've been thinking that a lot about myself lately."

She shot him a questioning look, but he waved it off as usual. He didn't want to think any more of how he'd found the deeper he dug into the Palmer case, the more he found that it was botched to high heaven. He'd think about it when and if he decided to take the case to appeal.

"Mom hates Roger. Roger hates her." She threw her hands up in frustration. "I don't know why I bother trying."

He waited a fraction of a second before responding. "I'll tell you why. Because you know she hates him."

Cara gave him a long sideward glance, but remained silent.

"Forgive me for saying it like this, but from what I've seen, you and Roger don't exactly seem like the ideal couple. No matter how ideal you say he is. What do you even see in him?"

"Roger is a-"

He waved his hand. "I know, I know, he's a *fine* man. You told me all that. Ruthie told me all that. But what else? Does he make you laugh?

Does he feed your soul? Does he take care of your heart?"

A flash of pain crossed Cara's face with his last remark. Just enough for him to read her true emotion. Bingo. She wasn't in love with Roger. And maybe she'd never been. His mood was lifting higher and higher by the moment.

She turned away, hiding her pained expression from him. "Maybe you've kept him in your life just to bug your mother?"

She twisted around to face him straight on. The fire in her eyes blazed. "I can't believe you're saying this to me? You think I'm with Roger just to get Mother Ruthie upset? Don't you think I'm capable of choosing my own companions?"

The fire in her was strong, but she wasn't angry, he noticed. She was merely hurt by his inference that Roger was a safe bet to drive her mother crazy.

His voice softened, and he took her hand in his. It was silky soft against his palm and the contact immediately took on an intimate feel. He looked at her cinnamon eyes and felt he could see straight through to the center of her being. It amazed him that they could be so close and yet so distant at the same time.

Their eyes locked and he wondered how he could ever tear himself away from her gaze. He didn't want to. He wanted to sit there and look at her, drown in the depths of her soft brown eyes.

Things had changed between them. Not just in those few short moments when he felt like this connection between the two of them was welded together. That was their friendship. But these new feelings were different. Like last night when she looked up at him while they were riding the carousel. In his mind, he knew this was the same Cara he'd known seventeen years ago. And yet, his feelings for her had changed. They'd grown deeper than he'd ever thought he was possible. They had an intrinsic connection that time had never been able to break.

Yet, something was wedged between them. Or rather *someone*.

Devin drew in a deep breath and brushed his thumb across Cara's fingers. These feelings were more than just friendship. There was no doubt in his mind about that now. It was only when he started to speak that he realized his breath was caught in his throat.

"I hate to see you settling for something for the wrong reasons, giving up your dreams," he said softly. "You deserve better than that."

Cara finally pulled her hand away, breaking the connection. Although the mid-day sun beat down hard on them, he suddenly felt cold.

Lifting herself up from the steps, Cara exhaled loudly. She walked a few steps down toward the picket fence and stared out at the ocean before swinging back to look at him.

"In Boston, everything made sense. I come down here for a few weeks and it seems my whole life is turned upside down."

"It happens. No one is immune. You just have to work through it."

He picked a splintered piece of wood off the stair tread, snapped it and tossed the two pieces to the sand. He had to admit he'd spent these past few sleepless night thinking about more than the Palmer case. He was thinking about re-writing his future. And every time he looked beyond leaving Cara, he didn't like it. Not one bit. That said more than any court transcript ever could.

She buried her head in her hands and chuckled wryly. "Every time I turn around I'm coming to you with something, Dev. You don't need to listen to all this crap on your vacation."

"You know you can always come to me."

"I think I've always known that," she said softly. Cara glanced at her watch and then rubbed it nervously. "I guess I should be getting back."

Devin heaved a sigh. "Getting ready for the big birthday party?"

She smiled and when she did, he couldn't help but smile, too. Her smile quickly vanished. "You're definitely coming to the party, right? I can only imagine what other surprises my mother has in store for me. Get a little champagne in Mom and she's liable to insist we get married on the spot with Roger as best man! I need you there tonight to make things bearable."

The past few days Devin had come to realize there was a lot he needed in his life, too. Most importantly, he needed the fanciful laughter of his best friend Cara.

"I've got to run, too," he said, pushing himself off the stairs. "I've got to go pick up Bruno at the Vet."

Cara's expression perked up. "You named the dog Bruno?"

"Do you think it fits?"

She smiled, walking backwards toward the gate. "Yeah. I think it fits great," she said softly. She waved before turning and walking toward the beach.

He watched her slip her sandals off her feet and dig her toes into the sand as she walked. As she made her way up the beach, his mind focused on her words. She needed him. There wasn't anything she could ask for that he wasn't willing to give her. That's the way it had always been.

He needed her, too. But Devin was sure Cara meant it in a different way.

She wanted his friendship.

He just wanted her.

Cara slipped on her pale pink cotton sun dress, thankful that the brief afternoon rain had cooled off the night air. Still, the thought of pantyhose was deplorable, so she chose not to wear any. From all the time she'd spent in the sun, her skin had a healthy glow. She chose only to wear a little mascara and pale lipstick for makeup.

After stepping into her white sandals, she descended the stairs to see if she could help her mother with any last minute details. She should have been looking forward to this festive occasion, but she wasn't.

She walked into the kitchen where her mother stood wearing an apron covering her dress. On her feet, swollen from the heat, she still wore her floppy slippers. Her face was the picture of contentment. Cara smiled inwardly. Ruthie loved catering to a crowd. Still, she had to wonder if her mother had any regrets choosing a family over her career.

"What can I do to help?" Cara asked.

"Nothing," Ruthie answered, smiling. "I've got it all under control. Maybe you can help your father?"

Instead of finding her father, she walked out to the back porch. The sun was just sinking behind the ridge of trees, casting long shadows across the yard leading to the beach. The humidity that had plagued them for the past week had eased some. She sat on the porch swing, waiting for Roger to finish dressing. Or working. She didn't exactly know what he was doing at the time. Odd. She had no idea what he was doing and they were living in the same house.

It was just as well Roger wasn't around. She needed time to think about what direction her life was going, and she couldn't do that if she had to paste on a smile and sound happy. Or worry about what fireworks would go off when Roger came face to face with her mother.

Within the hour, the house was filled with her parents' friends as well as old friends Cara hadn't seen in years. Somehow her mother managed to contact her assistant, Louise, for a list of Cara's friends from Boston. It kept her busy mingling. Since Roger knew most of her friends from the city, Cara was pleased when she looked over and saw that he was comfortably conversing with a group of people. Unfortunately for her, it left her more time to watch Penny, who was putting on an award winning performance cozying up with Devin.

She had to stop this. She had no business being jealous of Devin with another woman. But she was. And it was almost painful to watch. She waited until Penny left Devin's side to approach him.

As she walked over to him, her mouth was as dry as a cotton ball. When his lips lifted to a wide smile, her spirits lifted a notch and she actually felt her heart flip.

Devin looked too good for words. He wore a new pair of blue jeans and a white cotton shirt that glowed against his newly tanned skin. She noticed he wore no socks, just a pair of dockside loafers on his feet.

He leaned forward and whispered in her ear. "Having a good time?" He smelled of aftershave and beer and something more. His skin was warm and intoxicating and she had to fight to keep herself from drifting closer to him.

"Yes," she lied. Before she had the chance to say anything more, the room hushed. She turned around to find everyone staring at her.

Her father walked slowly into the room holding her birthday cake with all the candles set ablaze. As he made his way toward her, the crowd of people in the room gathered around her and everyone began to sing Happy Birthday.

She looked at their faces. They all wore smiles as they sang. But inside, Cara just wanted to cry. What the hell was wrong with her? This was her birthday and everyone was there in honor of her, for heaven's sake.

When the singing stopped, Devin said, "Make a wish, Cara." Everyone around her chanted his words, but all she could concentrate on was Devin.

Cara filled her lungs with air and then forced it out again, blowing out all of the thirty-five candles on her birthday cake. When she stood up straight and looked into the crowd, everyone clapped. She only wished she could do the same. She'd just wished for the one thing she could never have.

Devin.

Chapter Eight

Cara sank down into the wing chair next to the table full of colorfully wrapped presents just as Elsie took hold of the microphone. Karaoke music blared as her mother stood to the side, holding a camera, ready to capture the moment on film. Her father disappeared to the den with Larry from the hardware store.

And Devin disappeared to the back of the room as soon as Roger stood by her side. Penny immediately gathered up to his side. Although she didn't want to be, Cara was acutely aware of where Devin was at all times. Was it her imagination, or was he really avoiding her whenever Roger was around?

As Roger handed her the first gift to unwrap, she couldn't take her eyes off Devin. He slumped against the doorjamb, holding the glass of champagne her mother had just passed out to everyone for the toast.

"Cara?" She looked at Roger, who wore a look of bewilderment. "Aren't you going to open your present?"

Cara glanced down at her lap and realized she was holding a long black velvet jewelry box adorned with a thick white ribbon tied into a large bow. She didn't remember taking it in her hands. "Oh, yes, of course."

She tore open the card to find it was a gift from her parents, a strand of pearls. What followed next was an array of gag gifts given by some of her friends from Boston. The beautiful royal blue nightie, given to her by Louise with a note to "get a life" got the best response from everyone in the room.

Except from Devin. With Roger's quip remark to "put it to good use," Devin shifted uncomfortably, turning his attention away from all the hoots and giggles. Even from the distance, she could see the tightness in his jaw, his whole body for that matter.

Roger handed her his gift and kissed her lightly on the cheek. The box black velvet like the one her parents had given her, but much smaller. Her heart pounded furiously in her chest, drowning out the next wave of song coming from the speakers in the back of the living room. She didn't want to open it. It was so unexpected. Was Roger really going to ask her to marry him? And in front of all these people?

She cradled the box in her sweating palm for a long agonizing moment. She had the vague feeling opening the innocent looking package was the equivalent of opening Pandora's Box. One quick motion and it was done.

Relief washed over her. Her eyes focused on the single diamond centered elegantly in a black gold setting. Roger had given her a diamond pendant. Her smile couldn't have been bigger.

"I knew you'd like it," Roger said, misreading her expression. "I've been working with a jeweler for months now to find the perfect diamond for you."

"It's beautiful," she said, looking at the gift. "I'll treasure it always."

Now that the table was empty and the last gift was unwrapped, the crowd applauded. Standing up, Cara closed the box and handed it to Roger. She was about to thank the crowd, but Devin stopped her.

"There's one more," Devin called out from the back of the room. Her blood thickened when Penny brushed her polished fingers across his back.

"Really?" She turned toward the table where all the gifts had been placed. There was nothing on the white linen covered table but a balled piece of wrapping paper and ribbon that hadn't landed in the trash bag.

"Look underneath."

She pushed aside the cloth and looked underneath. She found a large box with a small card tucked between the stiff gold ribbon adorning it. With Roger's help, she reached down, picking it up and plunking it on top of the table. Cara opened the card and read the writing.

"There are some things just too precious to leave behind, Devin."

Her heart melted like warm honey when she looked up and saw his face. In a million years, she knew she'd never forget that soulful look Devin gave her. The distance between them seemed minimal now. She could almost hear his thoughts, his heartbeat. The fact that Penny was standing right next to him was suddenly of no consequence. Devin was with her at that moment, and no one else in the room seemed to matter.

One pull and the bow came undone, falling to either side of the box on the table. She lifted the lid and pushed away the tissue paper. Her heart melted and her lips trembled. She had to clamp her teeth down on her bottom lip to keep it from trembling.

"The wooden carousel," she whispered, holding back the tears threatening to break her control. She turned and looked at Devin and saw a shimmer of light in his eyes. More emotion passed between them in that moment than ever had during their entire friendship. It wasn't special just that he'd known how much she wanted this carousel. After all, it was just an object. But it was a gift from his heart and that was what mattered the most.

Moisture filled her eyes but she didn't care if anyone saw or thought her reaction was strange. She let her tears fall freely down her cheeks.

This was it, she realized. This was the very thing she'd been missing all along. She didn't need a man to take care of *things* for her. She needed someone to take care of her heart. And no one she had ever met in her life had ever done that better than Devin.

"I guess that about does it," Roger said, putting his arm around Cara.

With that single point of contact, Cara saw Devin's whole body stiffen. The precious moment between them had been shattered by one simple word. He grabbed a bottle of champagne from the bar and stalked out of the room. Penny followed on his heels.

"Thank you, everyone," Cara announced, forcing her lips to form a smile. Her hands trembled and her heart tore in two. Devin had left with Penny. Cara suddenly thought she'd die but she fought to hide her emotion from all the eyes bearing down upon her. "Please, there's plenty of champagne, so have fun."

"Happy birthday, honey," Harold said, reaching out to give her a hug.

"Thanks, Dad. Careful, your wires will come undone." She leaned forward and tugged on the wire coming from his pocket. "Who's winning?"

His face registered shock that he'd been found out, and he placed a finger at his mouth to shush her. Then he grumbled, "Damn Yankees."

If only he knew her mother had orchestrated the whole thing.

Roger was by her side again, yawning and scratching the back of his neck.

Cara took a deep breath. "Poison ivy still bothering you?"

"The way my skin looks, I feel like a burn victim. I've been thinking..." He averted his gaze and she knew she wasn't going to like what was coming next.

"You're going back to Boston," she said, sparing him.

He cocked his head to one side and exhaled. "I should probably see a specialist for this rash. It's getting worse."

She tried to act disappointed, but in the end, she lost the battle. This whole week had been one big farce. Roger's leaving somehow felt like a relief. "I'm sorry it's getting too much for you here."

His eyebrows darted up. "No, it's not that at all. Things have actually been...bearable."

She managed to laugh. "When you cocoon yourself in my father's den the way you do, how could it not be?" She took him by the hand. "We never did get around to going on that trip to Nantucket."

He squeezed her hand and began to say something, but his expression changed. "Why don't you go with Devin?"

A chill raced through her. No, the thought of being with Devin didn't leave her cold. Quite the contrary. But the fact that Roger seemed unaffected by her spending so much time with another man did. She didn't bother to ask him if he'd be jealous, because she already knew he wouldn't be. She quietly contemplated what that said about their relationship.

"Maybe."

Roger bent down and kissed her forehead. "I'm bushed. Do you mind if I call it a night?"

"No, of course not." She gave him a hug, but her arms felt empty.

As soon as Roger climbed the stairs, Ruthie sashayed over to Cara.

"Where on earth is Roger going?" she asked, handing Cara a fresh glass of champagne.

"To bed." And as if she felt the need, she added, "He's been working hard these last few days."

To Cara's great relief, Ruthie stifled a retort. Instead she said, "Devin was just looking for you. Did he find you?"

"No." Cara looked around the room but she saw no sign of Devin or Penny. Her stomach twisted into a tight knot. "Maybe he left."

"Oh, I don't think he'd leave without saying good-bye and giving you a birthday kiss." Ruthie's face was telling, leaving no room for misunderstanding her meaning.

Cara groaned, taking a generous sip of champagne. "I think he's saving that for Penny."

"Don't be too sure."

Ruthie reached into the box behind the bar and pulled out a full, uncorked bottle of champagne and two clean crystal glasses from the tray, holding them out to Cara.

"Why don't you go look for him?"

Cara didn't hesitate grabbing the glasses and the bottle.

She was nuts, Cara decided. Not her mother, but her. She'd become completely immune to her mother throwing Devin at her, but now she was actually following Ruthie's advice. Of course, she had no intention of acting on any of the wild feelings for Devin that had been haunting her. Roger was asleep upstairs and it just wouldn't be right.

Besides, Devin was her best friend. And right now that was what she wanted more than anything. Plain and simple.

Much to her relief, Cara found Devin alone. He sat on the back porch, one long leg lifted over the railing, the other foot touching the floorboards, his back pressed against the post. He was looking out at the ocean, lost in thought, clutching the bottle of champagne she'd seen him take from the bar.

"*Deja vu*," she said quietly, so as not to make him jump. "I seem to recall us doing this very same thing seventeen years ago on my eighteenth birthday."

His lips lifted to a slow, sexy smile she found irresistible. "You're just as beautiful now as you were then."

Her resolve melted. Devin had never talked like that to her before. It was a simple line, as old and used as they come, but hearing it from him in his deep, husky voice made it sound brand new.

"Thank you."

The sound of the waves crashing into shore roared around them. The gentle breeze coming in with the tide brought a pungent scent of salt to the night air. The silence between them was deafening. If she didn't do something—and fast—there was no telling what would happen.

"Where's Roger?"

"Turned in early. All this excitement was a little too much for him." She hesitated a moment. "I expected Penny to be hanging all over, ah, around you."

A number of emotions flashed across his face, disappointment, satisfaction, before it settled on relief. "She had to get her beauty sleep."

Cara sucked her cheeks in slightly to hide her own satisfaction. "What a shame. You've been keeping her up nights?"

His eyebrows furrowed. "What gave you that idea?"

The little gropefest I saw the other night might have something to do with it.

"She is a very attractive woman."

"Yes, if you want to make a career of it. Which she has. But that's not what I'm looking for."

"Really. What are you looking for, Dev?"

The heat in his eyes simmered as he gazed washed over her. This was not the look of a man hungry for his friend's advice. He was hungry all right, but in a primal way that made her whole body tingle. She was about to get devoured...and the thought of it made her tremble with excitement.

"That's what I came here to find out."

He took a deep breath, expanding his chest against his shirt, leaving Cara shivering with anticipation. The tight knot she'd felt all night begged to be released.

Devin lifted from the porch rail and advanced toward her, taking Cara's hand. A gentle breeze brought with it the scent of the sea intermingled with the scent of Devin's aftershave. He squeezed her hand, the contact immediately triggering a chain reaction that magnified her senses, leaving her pulse pounding.

"Let's go," he whispered against her ear, tickling her skin.

"Where?"

"I don't know. We'll figure that out when we get there." He grabbed his bottle of champagne and hers and turned toward the stairs.

"Wait. I can't leave my own birthday party," she said. Although she probably wouldn't need more than a little nudge to follow Devin.

"Yes, you can. *Deja vu*, remember? We did this on your eighteenth birthday."

Giddy excitement filled her. It felt just like something they use to do when they were kids. Which, for some strange reason, Cara found exhilarating.

She ran toward him. "Let's get out of here while we still have the chance."

Chapter Nine

Thirty minutes later, the two of them sat on the sand by a crackling campfire on the stretch of beach in back of Devin's cottage. Bruno stretched out on the sand, sleeping peacefully as Devin stroked his newly cleaned fur. Cara was well on her way to polishing off the first bottle of champagne.

She popped the cork on the second bottle and giggled when the bubbly flowed out the mouth and dribbled down her arm. So what if she was starting to feel the effects of her drink? It was her birthday, after all, and she with Devin. Just like old times. *Thank God, some things never change.*

"That's the whole point, Dev," she said, continuing the conversation they'd started. "Roger doesn't need me. No one needs me. I can come and go as I please, work as late into the evening as I want, and sleep til noon. Roger just want my companionship and asks absolutely nothing but that from our relationship."

"Somehow, it doesn't seem that simple to me."

The cool breeze swept in from the ocean, caressing her warm cheeks. "No, it is. And I like it that way."

"Then why have you been so down?"

Cara shot Devin a look. Damn, he looked too good stretched out on the sand. The wind whipped a lock of dark hair over his forehead, making him look incredibly sexy. One look and she almost forgot to tell him to stuff it.

She tucked her feet under herself and shifted, uncomfortable with the longing she couldn't seem to shake. She watched as he stretched out on the sand, looking up at the stars with his hands laced behind his neck. Bruno whined and lay snuggled up along the side of him.

Cara had a deep longing to do the very same thing. How could she not feel safe and warm curled up next to Devin?

"What about a baby? They're pretty demanding," he said. "That's something that was never part of your grand plan."

She sighed, her shoulders sagging. "I know. But somehow, that's different."

"How?"

"That's family. I mean, sure, I'm not a morning person, so this two o'clock followed by the inevitable five o'clock feeding scares me a little. That will eventually pass. And the demands of a child are different than the demands of a man."

"How?" he repeated. And she was beginning to get annoyed.

She turned her thoughts over in her mind a few times. Maybe it was the drink, but she couldn't come up with one valid reason to support her argument. Babies didn't care that their mommies were up late the night before working on a project and wanted to sleep in the next morning. A dirty diaper needed to be changed whether or not you had a business meeting with a potential client. Then there were doctor appointments and new shoes and clothes that had to be bought and...

Babies were demanding. Period.

But it *was* different. She just couldn't figure out how. And then she remembered her mood swings since she'd been home. Her parents were moving away and selling the house she had grown up in. Although they were still here, she was already missing family. Now that she'd tasted success in her professional life, she wanted to bask in the warmth of having a family of her own. Family meant at least two people and hopefully the addition of more.

She sighed heavily. "It's inevitable that when two people have a baby, the woman is always forced to give up her career over the man's."

"Says who?"

She shrugged and reached over to pour more champagne in Devin's glass. "Everyone I know. Look at my mother. She started her own catering business when she was eighteen. Everything was great until I came along. Then she quit."

"Maybe that's what she wanted."

"I don't know about that. You saw her tonight. She's never happier than when she's in a kitchen full of food, getting ready to serve a hundred people. And you see the way she caters to my father."

Devin rolled over and propped his head up on his palm, his elbow sunk deep into the sand. "Maybe she thought that her family was more important."

Cara sobered, looking down at the empty glass in her hand. Her head was spinning, and she fought to keep back the emotion waiting to spill out. "Maybe I'm afraid I'm too selfish and I won't."

Devin sputtered. "Knock it off. You're anything but selfish. Besides, it's not like years ago when the family roles were carved in stone. Lots of women work after having children and lots of men have taken an active role in raising their kids."

Cara poured champagne into her glass and lifted the glass to her lips. The sweet taste of the liquid was strong and the bubbles tickled her nose as she drank. Looking at Devin, she tried to imagine him as a father. She'd never thought of him that way before. But then again, she'd never thought of herself as the motherly type, either.

So many things about the last few days had changed her thinking. And it was scaring her to death. She just wanted to tell the world to stop and let her off. She wanted to keep what little she could count on locked in a bottle. No surprises. No more changes.

"Would you do it? Give up your career to stay home with a family?"

Devin's mouth flew open, but he didn't say anything.

She groaned. "Just as I thought."

"No, wait a minute. You're asking me to go from zero to ninety in a heartbeat. Who said only one has to give up? Marriage, family, that's all supposed to be a team effort. Who's to say both parents couldn't cut down their hours and work part time?"

"I can't picture you working part time."

A strange look crossed his face that she couldn't read, leaving him looking vulnerable.

"Why not?"

"You're the confirmed bachelor, remember?" Or so she'd always thought. So many things were changing around her, she couldn't keep up anymore. "You've always been full steam ahead. I just can't picture you slowing down."

"I'm think of jumping the train all together."

She almost choked on her champagne. "You?"

He gave a half grin. "You don't have to look so shocked. It's not that radical an idea. You're not the only one who has had a change of heart."

"I can't help it. Of all people, I thought that surely you would..." She took a sip of champagne and swallowed it hard. "What about that case you were researching?"

"That's part of the reason. But I've been wondering about things for quite some time. In law school, I'd heard about lawyers who get a sort of professional mid-life crisis after practicing about ten years, but I thought I was immune to it." He sighed. Clearly whatever it was that had brought him back home was weighing heavy on his mind. "I just don't know if I want to play the game anymore."

He looked so exposed. For a man of Devin's stature, that could mean death in his career. Appearance was everything. But seeing him this way didn't make her think of him as weak. Anything but. His conviction was strong as was his will. And that was something to admire. She always had.

"You always wanted to be a lawyer. And you're the best. What's changed it for you?"

"The definition of justice is beginning to get a little murky to me."

She laughed, mostly to help ease the tension lines on his face. "After a bottle of champagne, everything's murky."

Devin didn't laugh. His face was stone cold serious. This wasn't some idle thing he'd thought up to make her whining seem real. This was very real to him.

She stretched out on the sand, lying flat on her belly and supporting her upper body on her elbows. "So tell me," she began softly, "why is this Palmer guy different from all the others?"

"He isn't. He's just a normal everyday guy who happened to get himself caught up in a major mess."

"Then what's the problem?"

Devin hesitated a moment and exhaled a slow breath. "Justice was never about right or wrong."

She frowned.

He nodded his head. "Yeah. No one gives a rat's ass who's innocent or guilty, only what they can prove, what they can win. After a while, you stop seeing your clients as people. You stop feeling. And pretty soon you've gone so cold that you stop feeling about everything in your life. It's all just a game. Years go by and you start to wonder why you're still playing it. Or why you wanted to in the first place. It's like some roller coaster ride that never ends."

He reached over and stroked a wayward strand of hair from her face, igniting a flame as strong as the bonfire on the beach. His eyes focused on her lips, caressing them with a single look. She involuntarily moistened them with her tongue, imagining what it would feel like having Devin's lips pressed against hers. To feel his hands stroking her bare skin.

She needed space, but couldn't muster enough strength to move away.

It wasn't just that she knew he'd kiss her if she stayed still. She wanted Devin to kiss her. It wouldn't take much and she knew there'd be no protest from her, drunk or sober.

She sucked in a deep breath and sat up, trying to collect herself, trying to keep her thoughts on the subject matter and not on what it would feel like to fall into Devin's arms, melt in his touch right that second.

"You don't care if your clients are guilty?" she asked, forcing herself back to the topic of conversation.

"It's not my job to care about whether or not they actually commit the crimes they're accused of. That's up to a jury to decide. It's my job to make sure my clients don't go to jail. Period."

She made circles in the sand with her fingers, keeping her gaze focused on the circles instead of Devin. "And if they're innocent?"

He sputtered. "Please don't tell me you're naive enough to think that innocent people don't go to jail."

She looked at him then. "Okay, I won't."

"It's not about innocence, or money, or justice. It's about winning. It's about getting a fair shot at justice. That's what we're taught in law school. Everything else is secondary."

"You couldn't have always believed that. What about that case you took right out of law school? What was his name...?"

"Luther Wells." Devin remembered it all too well.

"Everyone thought he'd go to jail but you convinced the firm to take the case and you won."

Heat coiled in the pit of his stomach. That was the case that had made him what he was today. What used to give him pride, now left a bitter taste in his mouth. The guy had been guilty as sin and admitted as much from the day of their initial meeting. Back then, he didn't care. It wasn't a matter of guilt or innocence. The firm had already decided not to take his case. Too much negative publicity had surrounded it and they had been sure to lose.

But Devin had been young and green and had had a fire in his belly that couldn't be extinguished easily. He'd convinced the senior partners that he could use all the negative publicity and turn it around to his favor. They thought he couldn't do it, that he had been sure to lose. But he'd shown them all and it catapulted his career forward. Everything after that seemed like a blur now.

He stared into Cara's soft eyes and the shimmer of light from the fire cascading off the waves of her dark hair. Lord, she was beautiful. Being with her made sense out of all the indecision and unrest waging war within him.

He tossed a twig into the fire. "You talk about me like I'm some kind of hero."

"You were to Luther Wells."

He sat up and brushed the sand from his arm. She didn't get it. Unless you played the game and believed their mantra, how could you really?

Most people envisioned justice as right and wrong. But it wasn't. It was all too gray to be defined. If you were smart, you used that to your advantage. The best attorneys did.

"What is it about Palmer that's keeping you up at night? Why is it that you're thinking of throwing it all away."

"I don't think he got a fair shot at the system."

"Wasn't that for *his* lawyers to handle?"

"That's just the point, they didn't. I received a letter from Palmer asking for me to help him appeal. After reading the court transcript..." He let out a disgusted sigh. "His lawyer dropped the ball so many times I wonder if he even knows what it looks like."

It wasn't his place to question another lawyer's strategy, but the whole thing was ridiculous. He could have tried this case in his sleep and still won.

Wendall Palmer was just another guy trying to fight against the system. His lawyer wanted the easy way out, a plea bargain. Devin had seen it done many times, but Palmer would have nothing to do with it. He'd maintained his innocence and the evidence supplied was compelling enough to convince Devin, too.

"If he's innocent, it will all come out in the end."

Devin chuckled sardonically. "That's not the way it works. Palmer's lawyer had an obligation to give him the best defense money can buy whether or not he had a pot to boil rock soup in. The trouble is, Palmer doesn't even have that. And his lawyer seemed to have decided it wasn't worth fighting."

He sighed, wondering where this ethical dilemma had come from. "Every man deserves the best defense money can buy, even if he can't afford it."

"Now who's looking through rose colored glasses. Somewhere and at some time another guy is going to fall through the cracks. You can't possibly save them all, Dev. "

"You're right. I can't take on every case. But I can help some. Those that won't have a chance otherwise."

"What will you do?"

He gazed at Cara and grinned, his breath catching in his throat at the mere sight of her. It amazed him how incredibly sophisticated Cara was and at the same time, so very vulnerable. The night breeze tossed her hair about until it fell in tangles on her bare shoulders. She was beautiful. But then again, he'd always known that. He'd just forgotten how much effect it had on him.

"I'm going to have another drink," he said, lifting the bottle to his lips and sucking down the warm liquid.

His head was spinning, but not from the alcohol. He needed Cara. He wanted her. God, how he wanted her. And not just for a quick roll on the sand. What he was feeling now was that forever kind of love that made his head lift to the clouds. The kind of love he never thought he could possibly have room for in his life.

She flashed him a wicked grin, and she tore the bottle from his hand. "Gimme that. I mean it."

He did, too. He wanted to make love to Cara. It wasn't like it was some great revelation. Their first kiss all those years ago had rattled them both and he'd wanted to make love to you then, too. Even though they'd pushed those feelings aside for their friendship, they were genuine. He remembered that now.

Cara had been right about one thing. Back then, they had been too young and eager to take on the world. One of them would have had to compromise their dreams if they'd given in to the youthful passion they'd felt for each other. He saw it now reflecting back at him like an image in a mirror. If they'd made love then, it would have destroyed their friendship.

When his father died and he'd gone back to college, he'd purposely chosen not to call Cara. Not because he didn't need her—Lord, he needed her more than ever then—but because it was the only way to stop the clock and keep what they had preserved in time. And he and Cara had passed the test of time. This week proved that. His feelings for Cara were stronger now than they'd ever been.

One of them would have had to choose and it would have destroy the precious friendship they shared. But that was all behind them now. They'd both made a success of their lives professionally.

Although the thought of Roger touching Cara nearly sent him through the roof back at the party, Devin didn't believe Roger was any real threat to what was happening between him and Cara. And there was definitely something incredible happening between them. But he'd be damned if he could figure out what was wedged between them.

"Come on," Cara urged. "Tell me."

He flashed her a half grin. "Maybe I'll act as stud for you and become a house husband."

She giggled. "You'd last all of five seconds with a dirty diaper."

His heart plummeted. "You don't think I'd make a good father?"

She silently stared at him, her expression collapsing. He watched her as the flames from the fire danced in her eyes.

"I've been thinking about a lot of things these past few days. Nothing has made any sense. Except when I think of you and me."

Cara's eyes dropped to her hands and she nibbled on her bottom lip. "Us?"

"Maybe your mother has been seeing something that we've been afraid to."

"My mother sees a lot of things and I'm afraid of them all," she said wryly.

He chuckled, but Cara could tell that there was no humor in the tone. Devin was serious. And she was feeling too good because what he was saying was actually making sense. She tried to imagine her and Devin having a baby, making love...

But what was she thinking? What was *he* thinking? That was an undertow that would only serve to destroy their friendship.

He inched closer and she felt his heat as strong as the flames from the fire, even though they weren't touching.

"We're not kids anymore, Cara. We don't have to be afraid of what we're feeling."

"You're delusional," she sputtered, trying to keep her insides from humming with his nearness. He was joking, right?

She sat up and straightened her spine, clearing her throat. "I'm involved with Roger," she said, stating the obvious.

"Roger's not here, Cara. It's only you and me."

Devin was staring at her, hot molten desire simmered in his eyes and set her on fire. Maybe it was the drink, but he was completely transparent now. And he wanted her. She kicked herself for actually liking that fact, liking the way his eyes caressed her. What could she possibly gain by making love with Devin? They were friends. They'd just found each other again after all these years.

She dragged her gaze away, but not before she saw the hurt register in his eyes. She hadn't meant to hurt him. After all, they'd had too much to drink and emotions were flying high. Tomorrow morning, well after he dried off this wet night, he'd see that it was just the champagne talking. She wasn't about to risk losing their friendship over ridiculous talk of marriage and babies with Devin Michaels. Not after they'd just found each other again.

She sighed, feeling an ache deep inside, an ache of unfulfilled need. When she finally had the courage to look at him again, she saw that his expression had softened.

"Cara." His voice floated to her. She could barely hear it over the roar of the incoming tide. But she saw his lips move and knew he had called her name as if she could really hear it. Reaching out, he stroked her bare arm with his fingers, sending a blazing sensation racing through the rest of her body.

Devin pulled himself from the sand and held his hand out to her. Her head was spinning, but she knew it wasn't the champagne. Devin was going to kiss her. He knew it and so did she. Taking his hand, she lifted herself from the sand like she was walking on air and fell into his arms, pressing herself against the rock hard wall of his chest. With his arms wrapped around her waist, he felt good, too good for her to muster any resolve to pull away.

He didn't kiss her at first. His dark eyes, black from the night and his desire, gazed down at her until she thought he could see the center of her soul. Reaching up, he touched her lips with his fingers, making her shiver with anticipation.

When his lips finally crushed against hers, it was with a fury that matched the force of the ocean, and she rose to meet that fury head on. His mouth was hot and demanding, tantalizing and delicious. And she wanted all of it. All of him.

She started to pull away, half wanting to give in to her desire, half wanting to listen to that little voice of reason telling her she was making a mistake. But Devin held her tightly to his chest and in his arms, she gave in to her heart.

It would be so easy to give in fully. So wonderful to take the very pleasure they both wanted in each other.

Devin tangled his fingers in her hair and pressed her against his chest. She felt the urgency of his desire hard against her belly. His heart pounded against her ear with each labored breath he took.

"Devin," she said, pushing with the palms of her hands flat against his chest. His scent filled her head and belied any strength she thought she had to keep her distance. Catching her breath, she found the strength to take a few steps backward. She held her hand in the air in the hopes that Devin would keep his distance.

The ocean crashed around them and sounded as thunderous as the hunger that had her on edge, echoing in her head. The crescent moon was a bright line in the sky. What little light it cast was drowned out by the crackling fire.

What the hell was she doing? She was kissing Devin Michaels. And she was loving every second of it! Wanting more of him.

A strange sense of excitement intermingled with regret gripped her. She'd never felt this way with anyone before, least of all Roger. No one had ever made her head spin or her heart beat like a wild stallion on a run.

But Devin had.

"I won't say I'm sorry for kissing you." Devin's voice was rough and sexy, filled with a need she felt.

"We shouldn't have done that," she finally muttered.

Bruno's tail slapped on the sand, cutting into her thoughts. She looked at the dog, lazily reclined on the sand next to an empty impression that Devin's body had made, and imagine her impression right along side it.

"You felt that kiss just as much as I did and still do. It was just as powerful as when I kissed you on the carousel that Fourth of July."

He took a step closer and reached out to touch her arm, but she pulled away. The pained expression on his face when she did nearly broke her heart.

She averted her gaze. "And it is just as powerful seventeen years later. A flame like this never dies, Cara."

She cleared her throat and took a deep breath, hoping to find some strength when she swung around to meet his gaze. But when she did, she realized she'd found none.

"I can't do this, Dev."

"Why not. You and me-"

"No!" She held her face in her hands and shook her head. This wasn't suppose to be happening. All these feelings, whirling around her, completely out of control. She was out of control.

"Don't you see? We're drunk, Devin. I won't risk losing this friendship again because of a few too many pops of bubbly."

She had to get out of there. Not just because her whole body was numb from the champagne, but because it wasn't. She was very much alert and aware of every sensation Devin had managed to bring to life with his kiss. She wanted him, and if she stayed there much longer, she was going to forget her own name and make love to Devin right there under the stars.

"Don't run away from me," he said, his eyes almost pleading with her.

"I'm not," she said, picking her white sandals up from the sand. "I'm trying to keep us from making a bigger mistake if I stay. Tomorrow, you'll see that I'm right." She only hoped she'd feel that way, too.

Devin didn't follow her as she spun around and quickly made her way along the edge of the beach. She blinked hard to see through her tears until she could finally focus on the porch light of her parents' home. When she did, she began to run.

Placing one bare foot on the wooden porch step, she glanced up at the window of her brother Manny's room. It was dark. All the windows downstairs were dark, too. The party was over, everyone had gone home, and Roger was fast asleep.

Yes, she was sure Roger was sleeping like a baby. Unlike Devin, Roger wouldn't feel jealous of her spending time with another man. As she yanked on the screen door, she couldn't help but wonder what, if anything, Roger would have felt if he'd seen that kiss.

Chapter Ten

He'd been hit by a train.

Devin was sure of it as he held his throbbing head and fought to pry his eyelids open. It was the only logical reason for his head feeling as though it were crushed like a over-ripe cantaloupe. Not only had he had the lack of brains to polish off the rest of the champagne he and Cara been drinking on the beach, he'd slumped on the sofa with Bruno at his feet and polished off the last of the beer in the fridge. The sledge hammer hitting his skull was punishment for his stupidity.

Serves him right, going after Cara the way he had done in a drunken stupor. How could she take his feelings for her seriously if she thought all she was was a drunken roll in the sack? She deserved more than that. So much more than he'd given her last night.

That kiss. God, it still seared him to the core with its memory. How could he think a passion like that could dissolve with time? It had been like dynamite detonating inside him.

They'd always been friends as kids. In his memories of her, they'd always maintained that their relationship was based on friendship, even after that one scorching kiss they'd shared.

Damn, what an idiot he'd been! He'd been deluding himself all this time. If he was at all honest with himself, he'd admit that he wasn't falling in love with Cara now for the first time. He'd always been in love with her. Except back then, it scared him to death. It still scared him, but it was different. He wasn't a kid trying to take on the world anymore.

And Cara had grown into an impossibly beautiful, sexy woman.

He swung his legs off the bed until they hit the floor with a thud. Trying to steady himself, he buried his face in his hands, shielding the light from his eyes. God, his head hurt.

Damn champagne, damn beer, damn...*Roger.*

His already aching gut twisted. He'd never felt this way about any woman he'd been involved with before. He was always much too busy to care whether the relationship lasted beyond being a simple distraction to his work.

But this wasn't just any woman. This was Cara. And there were no words to describe what she meant to him.

Cara had said she wanted to save their friendship. But deep inside, he knew she wanted him as much as he wanted her. They would have made love last night and it would have been wonderful. And instead of waking up with a colossal hangover, he'd be cradling Cara's warm naked body in his arms right now.

Why was she being so stubborn? Why couldn't he get her to believe that everything about them was a perfect match?

He couldn't do this alone. No, he'd have to employ some heavy hitting troops to win this battle. The best in the field. And he knew exactly who to go to for help.

Cara sat on the edge of the bed, still nursing a cup of coffee and hoping the two aspirin she'd taken would hurry up and kick in. "Are you sure you want to leave?"

"Yes," was all Roger answered.

She sighed. She'd hoped that sleep would have changed things for both of them. But it hadn't. She was glad this week with Roger was over.

"Don't be disappointed. We can go to Nantucket another time. Maybe after your parents leave for Florida." The little snicker in his voice didn't escape her.

"What is that supposed to mean?" she shot back defensively.

"Simply that I think this mood you've been in will finally pass after your parents move. That's all."

His explanation did nothing to assuage her irritation. Neither did the aspirin she'd taken a half hour ago.

"No, it won't," she huffed, instantly regretting giving up precious air as the room began to spin. Pressing her fingers to her temples, she added, "And I'm not moody, either."

Roger tossed his shaving kit in his suitcase. "Call it what you want, but I'll be glad when there's a little distance between you and your family."

She glared at him, unable to believe what he'd said.

Roger cocked his head to one side and smirked. "It's not like you've got the normal, garden variety family, Cara. Even your brother became a priest to escape the wrath of Ruthie Dearest."

"He did not!"

"Let's face it, most people have parents that play bingo and squawk about their neighbors at the parish hall dance. Your grandmother goes deep sea fishing every chance she gets, your father is relegated to watching the baseball game at the hardware store and your mother has been making baby booties for her grandchildren since you were born." He laughed and shook his head. "You have to admit it's a bit odd."

"What's wrong with that?"

His eyes flew open wide and he propped his hands on his hips as if in disbelief. "If you have to ask, then you've been around their influence too long."

Her blood was like ice flowing through her veins. How had she managed to push aside his feelings for her family for so long? Did he really think she thought so little of them like he did? "Their influence is what made me the woman I am today," she scowled.

"You're nothing like your family, I'm happy to say."

"I *am* my family. And I'll probably cry like a baby on the day that U-haul takes them to Florida."

She slammed her coffee mug on the night stand, sloshing liquid over the rim, and knotted her arms across her chest.

"You're such a snob, Roger. I can't believe I never saw this before."

"Exactly. And you say you're not moody?"

"I'm defensive. And why shouldn't I be when you talk as if I've got *The Munsters* for a family? I'll admit that they're sometimes a bit off-"

"A bit?" he challenged.

"But they love each other. They're committed to each other and they aren't afraid of that."

"What's that supposed to mean? What about us? We're committed to each other and we don't act whacko."

"Are we?" she asked, deciding to let the whacko comment slide. Given her hangover, she only had so much fight in her and she needed to save it for the important issues.

His mouth dropped open and he nodded. "So that's what this is all about. You want a commitment."

He smiled, but instead of having its usual effect, Roger just looked smug. And she wanted to wipe that self righteous smirk right off his face.

"If you wanted to get married, why didn't you just say something?" he said. "If you need a piece of paper to prove to yourself and your family how we feel about each other then fine, we'll get married."

Cara couldn't believe her ears. This was the last thing she wanted.

She'd been fighting this demon all week and it still managed to drag her to the ground.

"I, ah, don't know." Did she really need proof that he loved her? She thought back on her behavior these last few days, wanting him to be jealous. She had been acting irrational. She'd tried to reason that she was being overly emotional about her birthday, seeing Devin...

She'd foolishly thought that Roger would show some kind of emotion, jealousy for her being with Devin. It wasn't fair of her to want that, but she couldn't help it. Everything about her relationship with Roger had remained steady. There'd been no surprises, no excitement at all.

All Devin had to do was look in her direction and the earth seemed to tilt on its axis. Heat flamed her cheeks with the thought of their kiss. It pretty much rocked her world. If she hadn't had the good sense to leave, Lord only knows what would have happened.

Her heart pounded in her chest. She knew exactly what would have happened. She and Devin would have made love. And it would have been wonderful. No doubt about it.

She felt the depression on the bed as Roger sat down next to her. Taking her hand in his, he said, "Why don't you take some time to think about it."

She nodded and flitted a quick glance at him. Yes, she had a lot of thinking to do. Mostly about what she wanted and where her life was headed. "Yeah, we need some space."

Devin stood frozen in the middle of the kitchen floor, holding a tea pot filled with boiled water in one mittened hand and a plate of Danish in the other. Devin could hardly believe his ears.

"Who's getting married?"

"You and Cara," Ruthie announced. She picked up the mug he'd just placed in front of her and dipped her tea bag in the boiling water, bobbing it up and down. "Well don't act so surprised. It's not like I've been keeping my intentions a secret. When I called you in Manhattan I told you exactly what I was planning. I don't know why you and Cara sound so shocked."

He stood there, completely dumbfounded, although he was hard-pressed to know why. This was exactly the kind of thing he would expect from Ruthie. But unlike Cara, he wasn't immune to it.

Ruthie stood up, took the tea pot from his hand. "Let me take that,

Devin. You look completely unnatural."

She dropped the kettle on the stove and swung around.

"Oh, and don't worry. I called your mother to invite her, but..." She bit her bottom lip. "She was a little upset you didn't call her yourself, so I smoothed things over and gave her all the details."

"Which are?"

"You and Cara are getting married on Labor Day."

"That's it?"

"Uh-huh. Don't worry. She's just as happy as I am." Ruthie sat down and turned her focus to the steeping tea, squeezing the excess liquid from her tea bag and acting as if all this was perfectly normal.

Yes, he called Ruthie to ask for guidance on how to handle this situation with Cara. Devin knew she had something up her sleeve, but he'd never dreamed she'd gone this far.

"And when were you planning to tell me this hoax of a wedding you've been planning was a real wedding?"

She looked at him innocently over the rim of her mug. "When you were on my side. Which is, I hope, the reason you called me here this morning."

He laughed, a rolling guttural sound that turned into a deep belly laugh he couldn't get under control. He turned and hunched over, resting his hands on the counter, trying to compose himself.

"I'm so glad you aren't angry," Ruthie said, smiling brightly.

Wiping the laughing tears from his eyes with his palms, he said, "You're a woman after my own heart, Ruthie."

"Yes, as long as that heart meets up nicely with my daughter's."

He sank into the kitchen chair opposite hers. A sobering thought clutched him. "There's only one problem."

"Which is?"

"She doesn't want me. She loves Roger."

Ruthie cocked her head to one side and rolled her eyes. "You don't really believe that, do you?"

After the way she'd kissed him on the beach, the way she gazed up at him with those big brown eyes of hers, he would have sworn she wanted him. And yet, there was *something* wedged between them.

"I don't know," he muttered.

She clanked her mug on the table. "Well, I do. And the fact that Roger is no longer in the picture just goes to prove that I am right."

"Roger's gone?" This was getting interesting.

"He packed his bags and left before breakfast this morning."

Although it wasn't her kitchen, Ruthie cleared the table of the mugs and Danish and brought them to the counter. She turned on the sink's faucet and added a dopple of dish soap.

"You don't have to do that," he said, knowing she was going to clean his dishes anyway, because that was just Ruthie's way. Unlike Cara, he didn't find it annoying, just amusing.

She shooshed him with her hands. "I'll only be a minute. You sit and think about what you're going to do to bring my daughter around."

He sank deeper into the chair. "I have no idea. That's why I called you."

She smiled her pleasure. "Remember, all is fair in love. Roger has opened a window, now make it into a door. Give Cara some space. But only for another day or two. Have you ever been to Nantucket?"

"No."

"It's simply breathtaking." She leaned against the counter as soap suds rose in the sink behind her. "They have those beautiful quaint Inns along the beaches. Very romantic."

She turned off the water and submerged her hands in the basin.

"Make sure you get a room with a sunset view. The morning sun makes it so hard to sleep in after a long romantic evening."

He couldn't believe what he was hearing. After refusing to let her thirty-five year old grown daughter share a room with a man she'd had an ongoing relationship with, Ruthie was practically giving him her blessing to sleep with Cara.

He loved the idea.

Three days had passed since Cara's birthday party. Two days had passed since Roger had left for Boston. But it seemed like another lifetime since Cara had last seen Devin. She'd thought of taking a walk by the cottage to see what he was up to, but had always managed to talk herself out of it. She had a lot to think about. She wanted a family. Her own family was leaving. But what weighed most heavy on her mind was Devin and how they would salvage their relationship after the searing kiss they'd shared.

Instead of thinking, she found herself engrossed in helping her parents pack for the move to Florida. The house had been sold and she was fighting her own conflicting emotions on a minute by minute basis, trying to imagine some stranger hanging pictures on the walls and living in *her* home. Every memory she had was stored between these walls. Each item she wrapped in bubble wrap had a story to it that she told herself again, as if she had to to keep the memory alive.

And Devin was there, too. So much of the memories she'd drawn on in her adult life revolved around that last summer when Devin was a staple here.

She tore a piece of tape out of the dispenser and applied it to the cardboard box she'd finished filling just as Elsie walked into the kitchen. Even with her frosted salt and pepper hair, she looked a lot younger than Cara felt. She was dressed in a skin tight coral wetsuit. Even with her silver-blue hair, she looked a lot younger than Cara felt.

With a jubilant smile, Elsie said, "I'm off to go parasailing with Albert."

"Parasailing? I know you really like him, Grandma, but isn't parasailing a little dangerous for...you know."

Elsie penciled eyebrows stretched high on her forehead. "Someone my age, dear?"

That's exactly what Cara had been thinking, but not wanting to hurt her grandmother, she stopped short of saying it.

Elsie simply chuckled. "Never you worry, Cara. Albert has wonderful aim."

Cara snorted. "I can't believe you're having an affair with a man who's Daddy's age."

"What woman wouldn't want to have an affair with a young virile man? Besides, someone around here ought to be having sex. It might as well be me. Why don't you join us?"

Cara stopped in mid-motion and sighed. "I think I'll pass."

Elsie's penciled eyebrows stretched high on her forehead. "Suit yourself. But for heaven's sake don't go moping around the house all day again. You're much too young. Besides, you can't blame it on a hangover forever."

"I'm not moping," Cara shot back defensively.

"Call it what you like, but you only have a few more days vacation. You said you wanted to go to Nantucket. Why don't you ask Devin if he wants to go with you?"

With the mention of Devin's name, tears filled Cara's eyes.

Elsie dragged a vinyl covered kitchen chair next to Cara and sank into it, taking Cara's hand. Her tone was soft and gentle as she spoke. "*Mia*

Cara, what's troubling you so?"

Cara puffed her cheeks. She suddenly felt like a little girl with a skinned knee. "For the first time in my life I have no idea what I'm doing."

Elsie chuckled long and loud. "It seems to me the answers have been dropped in your lap. All you have to do is pick them up."

"That's easy for you to say." She puffed her cheeks. "He asked me to marry him."

Elsie smiled warmly and squeezed Cara's hand. "That's wonderful news, dear."

"I haven't said yes yet."

"Why on earth not? You love him, don't you?"

Cara sighed. She knew the answer was no. Although she cared about Roger, she wasn't in love with him. She was in love with Devin.

Elsie gave her a gentle hug. "If you want to know what I'd do-"

Cara perked up. "Yes, I do."

"Marry him."

Despite her foul mood, she felt a smile tug at her lips. "That sounds strange coming from you."

Elsie laughed, but her eyes held a bittersweet twinkle. "You were too young to remember your grandfather. We loved each other passionately. There's nothing you don't do to be with a man you love."

"Yeah, I know. Look at Ma. She gave up everything, her career, her dreams, everything to take care of us."

Elsie frowned. "Wherever did you get an idea like that?"

"I grew up here. I was privy to it first hand."

"If that's what you saw then you mistook your mother giving up her life for choosing what she wanted the most in the world. Her family."

"But I always thought—"

"No, you assumed. This family was and is your mother's dream. She chose her lot in life. Just like you've chosen yours. Just like I've chosen mine. You assumed wrong."

Cara closed her eyes. She hadn't assumed everything. She hadn't assumed that Devin would have given her a kiss so passionate the other night on the beach that her body still reeled with its intensity. If she had known the outcome of that evening, the effect his very touch would have had on her, she would never have willing gone with him.

Elsie placed her hand, more worn from age and *wisdom*, over Cara's. "I know how tiresome things can be with your mother. Remember, I raised her. But she only acts the way she does because she wants so very much for you to be happy. Besides all you young folk have it backwards. When you're young, you do it right and get married. When you're my age, you can live in sin."

Cara couldn't help but laugh.

"Marry him," Elsie said softly, a twinkle of emotion sparkling her eyes. "Devin is a good man."

Cara couldn't keep her jaw from dropping in shock. "I wasn't talking about Devin."

"I thought you just told me Devin asked you to marry him."

"Roger is the one who proposed."

Elsie tilted an eyebrow and scowled. "Fine Roger?"

Cara crisped. "Yes."

Pushing her sunglasses up the bridge of her nose, Elsie shook her head. "And everyone is afraid I'm the one with Alzheimer's."

"Come on Grandma. I'm serious."

Elsie shrugged and winked. "I didn't get to be my age without being caught in a love triangle...or three."

"So what do you suggest?"

"You're a smart woman," she said, picking up an empty box from the table and tossing it to the floor. "I say it is high time you get out of this house and take some time for yourself. You've been talking about going to Nantucket since you came home. Why not go with Devin? Go as friends, if nothing else. If that's all you are to each other, than what's the harm?"

As Elsie waltzed out of the kitchen, sunglasses propped on her nose, Cara had the vague feeling she'd been nothing more than a coward.

Devin killed the ignition and sat numb in the front seat of his car, staring at the most wonderful sight he'd seen in days. Cara was waiting for him on his front porch. His groin tightened immediately with the memories of how he'd held her in his arms the other night. How her soft body felt so right next to his and how much he'd wanted to take that soul shattering kiss they'd shared to the next level.

Bruno slapped his tail against the leather seat, peering up at him. Reaching over to the passenger's side, Devin released the harness that kept the dog safely secure and grabbed the leash. "Come on, boy."

The dog quickly obeyed, hobbling on three legs while favoring the bandaged one.

Cara waved. He could tell she was nervous by the way she kept dipping her gaze and fiddling with her fingers. Damn, he hated that. There was no reason for either one of them to feel anything uncomfortable with each other.

He padded up the brick path, his legs suddenly feeling like Jell-O.

"Roger working?" he asked, feigning ignorance.

Her sweet lips twitched. "Yeah, but in Boston this time."

Cara bent down and opened her arms to greet the dog. Bruno rose to the occasion by pushing back his ears and wagging his tail against her as she lovingly caressed his coat.

Standing up and wiping her hands on her shorts, she said, "You haven't been around."

"I didn't know you'd come by. Why didn't you leave a note or call?"

"I figured you might be busy."

He smirked, knowing she was referring to Penny. "I've been working on some paperwork for the Palmer case."

She grinned. "Same old Devin. I knew you couldn't stay away from Law."

Bruno barked, calling Cara's attention. She leaned over and stroked him behind the ears.

"I found his owners."

She snapped her head up. "You did?"

"Yeah, I got a call from Dr. Schroeder. Seems his owners were on vacation here over Fourth of July weekend. He got spooked by the fireworks and ran off. They weren't able to find him before they left, but they've been calling around, trying to find him ever since. His name is Duke."

"Duke." Cara lifted the dog's muzzle to get a good look at his mug. "You look like a Duke."

Duke wagged his tail harder as if liking the sound of his own name after all this time. Cara stroked behind the dog's ears. "So when are they picking him up?"

"This afternoon sometime. They're driving down from Vermont."

Cara leaned into him, wrapping one arm around his waist and giving a gentle squeeze. "You're going to miss him, huh?"

What he'd missed was Cara and now that she was in his arms, he didn't want to let her go. He'd missed everything. The way her sweet scent clung to him whenever she was near. The way his body involuntarily responded when they touched. The way she felt so perfect in his arms right now.

He waved her off with a shrug. "Nah. It's just a dog."

She eyed him and gave him a gentle jab in the ribs. "Stuff it, Dev. You're going to miss this little guy."

The only thing he'd truly miss was Cara, as soon as she left for Boston. It was now or never for them.

She was fiddling with her fingers again as if she were having a hard time saying something. "Are you chained to your paperwork or are you free to take some time off?"

"What did you have in mind?"

She drew in a nervous breath. "Since Duke and Roger has left us orphaned, how about going to Nantucket?"

Chapter Eleven

Right from the moment the ferry slipped into Steamboat Wharf, Cara knew that things would be all right between her and Devin. The flurry of activity from the tourist at the pier fed the anticipation she'd had in coming to Nantucket. Being with Devin just made it all the more special.

With the ocean breeze swirling all around them, Cara felt the emotional tension that had plagued her for weeks ebb away. She only wished the sudden rush of excitement she felt every time she captured one of Devin's smoky-eyed gazes would fade. She was sure her reaction to his touch—an innocent brush of his hand across her back, pushing a stray lock of hair out of her face—would give her away.

But for now, she'd be thankful that she and Devin were getting back on track. Her rattled nerves had calmed as they swam at Madaket Beach. Located on the western-most portion of the island, Madaket was famous for its beautiful sunsets.

They talked of her family and her shop in Boston. But mostly, they just enjoyed the laughter and the easy feeling of being together. It was a perfect end to an otherwise stressful vacation.

With the sinking bronze sun behind them, they pedaled back from Madaket along the dusty bike path at full speed. A certain sadness that their day together was coming to an end consumed her, but Cara pushed strong to make it back to the wharf in time to return the bicycles and make the last ferry to Woods Hole.

Devin had suggested to her they get a room and stay a few days, but she insisted they go home. While it was easy and carefree to be out in the sun with Devin, she didn't trust herself to be alone with him in the quiet evening, where the romance of an exotic island would surely betray her strength. Exerting force on the pedals, Cara tried to convince herself her vigorous push was because she had to keep up with Devin, not keep unbidden memories of their kiss on the beach from creeping into her thoughts. But he lagged behind.

"Come on. We're going to miss the ferry." Darting a glance back, she noticed Devin was more than a bike length behind her. "Get the lead out, Dev-" *Where was he?*

She squeezed the brake on her handle bars until the bike came to a screeching halt. Straddling the bike with her sneakers planted firmly on the ground, she twisted back in horror.

Devin's mountain bike lay wrenched in the middle of the dusty path. All she saw of Devin was his legs lying flat on the gravel, his upper body buried in a patch of high grass. She bolted to him, running alongside the bike. All the while her heart was buried in her throat.

As Cara reached him, she threw her bike aside and dropped to the ground beside him, digging her knees into the gravel.

"What happened?" she gasped.

Blood, God, look at the blood dripping down his forehead! Fear gripped her like a vice squeezing her chest. He wasn't moving. With a shaky hand, she touched the angry spot just above his eye and lightly brushed away a dusting of gravel embedded on his skin. He groaned and her heart lifted a notch.

"Talk to me, Devin," she begged, just short of hysteria.

His eyes drifted open and blinked from the sun. It was hazy, but Devin finally made out Cara's form hovering above him.

"Are you okay?" Her voice was far away but the sweet scent that was uniquely her drifted to him, making his senses come alive. He knew even before she touched his face with her soft fingers, that she was right beside him.

"Yeah...I just got the wind knocked out of me," he mumbled, trying to lift his head. With the motion, he felt the ground tilt and he slumped back. "This isn't going to work."

"Give yourself a minute." Through squinted eyes, he saw Cara twist around frantically, as if she were searching for something, someone. "I have to get you to a hospital."

An hour later they were sitting in an emergency room that looked like all the others he'd ever seen. Bright lights hummed and the sterile stench of antiseptic hung in the humid air.

Holding his bloodied shirt to the sight of his wound, Devin was vaguely aware of the admissions nurse talking to him. He and Cara sat in the seats at the front desk, answering questions the woman then typed into the computer file. With his head throbbing, much like he'd had the day of his lethal hangover, he was happy when Cara took charge of the small talk.

"It's gonna rain tonight. I can feel it in my bones," the woman said.

Cara forced a smile. "You know the unpredictability of New England weather."

The nurse chuckled. "If you wait a minute, it'll change. Reason for visit?"

"Exploding head," Devin muttered, dropping the soiled shirt he'd been using to stop the bleeding.

The nurse snapped her head up and studied him. "Hmm. I'd say so." She typed a little and asked, "Dizziness?"

"Not anymore."

"Disorientation?"

"No."

She leaned over the desk and asked Cara, "Is this your first time to the island?"

Picking up his head, Devin felt a pain stab behind his eye and shielded it from the white desk lamp causing him harm. Burying his head in his hands, he muttered, "Can we just get this over with, please?"

"Cuts on the head like yours look a lot worse than they really are because they're bleeders. Next of kin?"

He was about to speak, but was cut off when Cara responded.

"Cara Cavarlho," she told the woman.

A warm sensation spread through him that settled in his chest, gripping him with tender emotion. After all their time apart, Cara thought of herself as his kin, his family. He knew he felt this connection to Cara that was so unbelievably strong, he didn't need blood or legal papers to define it. But knowing that Cara felt that way too made it just that much stronger. It was the most wonderful thing he'd ever heard her say.

It hadn't taken more than an hour for Devin to be examined and have his wound stitched. Cara disappeared sometime before the emergency room doctor made seven stitches to the gash on his forehead. When he was done, he informed Devin he was free to go. All he had to do was find Cara.

He was just pulling on his blood stained T-shirt when Cara made it back to the examining room.

"Where did you run off to?"

She caught one sight of the soiled shirt and grimaced. "We're going to have to get you another shirt."

"Unfortunately, the gift shop is closed and probably a lot of the shops in town, too."

"We have bigger problems than getting you a shirt. I've been on the pay phone, trying to see if I could find us rooms for tonight."

He couldn't help but smile. "You changed your mind about staying the night."

"Since the last ferry back to the mainland is long gone, the decision was made for me. The only problem is, I can't find a single room." She threw her hands up in frustration. "I have no idea where we're going to sleep."

Flinging the hospital gown he'd been wearing to the bed, he said, "We'll find something."

She laughed. "I'm glad you think so. I've just been told it's against the law in Nantucket to sleep on the beach and this is the busiest time of the year. I've spent the last twenty minutes on the phone and there isn't a room available on the island."

He shrugged. "People are always booking rooms and canceling at the last minute. Don't worry about it."

Forty-five minutes later they reached the Graystone Inn. They'd walked the cobbled stone path to the front door, walking their bikes along side of them.

The Graystone Inn was located just off the main drag. While not along the beach like some of the other Inns, it's charm and grace was striking. Mr. and Mrs. Patterson, the owners of the Inn, greeted them as soon as they walked through the door. Devin took charge of inquiring about a vacancy with Mrs. Patterson, while Cara spoke to Mr. Patterson about returning their bicycles to the bike shop at the wharf. When Mr. Patterson assured her that he would return the bikes for them, Cara found Devin in the main foyer.

Devin lips lifted to a smile as he dangled a room key from his fingers. "I got the last room."

Too relieved to care about the details, she wasted no time following Devin upstairs to the privacy of their room. *Their one room.*

Devin slumped back on the goose down pillow to ease his throbbing head. This wasn't exactly how he had envisioned spending this night alone with Cara. In his dreams, he'd pictured them deciding that being together was what they both wanted and Cara tossing all this nonsense about just remaining friends aside. He'd imagined a moonlit night where they would sit on the balcony and sip champagne. He'd lead Cara to the four poster bed and carefully strip every stitch of clothing from her body.

And they'd make love over and over again until the sun rose over the bay.

Instead, he lay on the bed as if he'd been bowled over by a bulldozer. Cara sat in a wing chair by the fireplace with her legs draped over the armrest. There was no romantic fire lit and no champagne chilling in an ice filled urn. She stared into oblivion as if she were deep in thought, her expression clouded and unreadable.

If she were truly happy with her relationship with Roger, Devin would never attempt to come between them. Except, deep down he knew in his gut that she wasn't.

More than a few times he'd looked at her during the day, only to find that she'd been gazing at him. He'd wondered what she thinking. Wondered if the memory of their kiss on the beach still haunted her the way it did him. Is that what she was thinking about now?

Lord, he hoped so. He couldn't stand to think of being in this alone.

His mission was clear. This was his last chance to make Cara see that *he* was the man to be holding her each night and nuzzling her each morning. Labor Day was only a few days away. After that, Cara was sure to go back to her life in Boston. Without him. He couldn't let that happen without her knowing exactly how he felt.

There was still so much to tell Cara. Not the least of which was his plan to move back to Westport for good. But there was still time to talk about all of that. First, he needed to know if she'd have him at all.

Cara forced herself from the wing chair she'd been slumped in and padded to the French doors leading to the balcony. It was raining, she realized, when she heard the rhythmic cadence of drops on the window panes. Neither the heavy rain nor the ceiling fan could assuage the humidity. There was no thunder or lightning anywhere, except deep in her heart.

She thought about telling Devin about Roger's marriage proposal. She hadn't thought about it all day, and she didn't want to. Today she'd been too happy being with Devin today to allow any of the uncertainty plaguing her to intrude.

It had been easy during their day together. Being with Devin was easy. Of course, that was when she thought they were going home to their own separate beds, not nestled in a quaint island Inn on a stormy night with only one bed. The unbidden feelings for Devin she'd tried to push aside all day had found a welcome home in this cozy room. She couldn't push past them any longer.

The sound of the rain dancing on the window pane was surreal, almost whispering to her to reach out to Devin. *You love Devin. Turn around and tell him you love him. I love you, Devin.*

The creak of the mattress caused her to angle back and look at him. God, he looked so good leaning up in bed, propped up on his elbow. The crisp white pillow case glowed against his tanned skin, golden bronze from their day in the sun. She could almost feel the hard lines of his chest beneath her palm, the swirls of his chest hairs tickling her fingers.

Devin swung his long legs over the side until they hit the floor. His smoldering gaze captured her eyes and waged a war of emotions inside her.

"Does your head still hurt as badly?" she asked softly.

"The aspirin finally kicked in."

She noticed the tension lines on his face had smoothed. She'd been so frightened seeing him lying on the ground... "What you said back at the hospital, about being my next of kin. Why did you say that?"

She took a quick breath and thought a minute. She hadn't given it any thought at all at the hospital. "I don't know. The nurse asked and I just said it."

He swallowed visibly. "After all these years, you think of me as your family."

She frowned. "Of course. It's impossibly for me to think of you any other way."

"Me, too. I think I've always thought of you and Westport as my real home." He inhaled a deep breath, expanding his chest. "I've decided not to go back to Manhattan, Cara."

Her eyes widened in disbelief. "Law, too?"

He shook his head. "The firm, yes. But not law completely. I still don't know what I'll do. Maybe I'll teach some classes. Maybe just take on the cases I believe in when it feels right. I've got time to decide."

She puffed her cheeks, trying to comprehend this new revelation, this new Devin.

He absorbed the space between them, but didn't touch her. For that she was glad. She didn't know how much control she had left.

Planting his hands deep in his pockets, he asked, "Do you remember my father?"

Regret tugged at her heart. "Not much."

"Unfortunately, neither do I. Except for that last summer before he died, I never really saw him. He was always working on some project. Something that always kept him from coming away with us for the summer or being there for anything that was important in my childhood."

He sighed heavily, seeing the pattern he learned early on had paved the way for him to follow.

"I don't want that, Cara. When I have children, I want to be there to watch them grow and help them achieve all they can. Or be there to brush off their knee when they stumble and fall. I want them to know me. That'll never happen if I stay on the track I've been running. My father was a good man, but I never knew him. We never shared much of anything. I don't want to wake up some day and realize the best part of my life was lived without me."

Cara didn't say a word. She turned toward the sparkled drops of water running down the window.

"This time away has done me a lot of good. I don't want to play the game by their rules anymore. I want to live by mine."

Her knees went weak with his touch as he gently tugged at the hair band holding her ponytail in place. With long lingering strokes, he combed his fingers through her hair, sending shivers down her spine. She leaned with her back against his chest and felt the energy sizzle between them. She didn't have to look at Devin to know what she'd see. She could feel it. Inside she was dying, thinking about what could be. And wanting it just as much.

"*Mia Cara*." He breathed her name in a voice that was mysterious, seductive, calling out to her in words that weren't spoken.

She couldn't breathe. She couldn't think. Cara had foolishly thought that this time with Devin would help make all the craziness of her life seem clearer. What a joke! After that night on the beach, she didn't think anything could rattle her. But she was wrong. Just being with Devin was enough to make her entire body shudder like ice in a crystal glass.

"It would be so easy for us to make love, Devin," she said, pressing her forehead against the glass, the cold pane sending a chill through her hot skin. "But what then?"

His deep rumbling chuckle enveloped her from behind as he hooked his arms around her. "We'd be a real family. A house, kids, the whole deal. We'd make an awesome team, don't you think?"

Devin's words echoed in her head. *We'd make an awesome team. We'd be a real family.* God, how she loved the idea of being with Devin. Making babies with him. Making love with him.

This change that had come over him was so drastic. Could he really be happy not driving himself in his career? Could she?

It all sounded so wonder now. It always did in the beginning. But after a time, Devin would put his career before hers and expect her to choose between family and her career. Just like her Louise. Just like her mother.

It would be easy, so easy to fall into bed with him and give in to the passion that was consuming her. And making love with Devin would be great. No doubt about it. But it would change everything. And what would be the cost?

Their friendship, her mind told her. They'd lost it once because of ambition and drive. If they took this step forward, there'd be no going back. They'd be lovers, not just friends. If it didn't work out, they could never go back to the friendship they'd had.

Devin's face was drawn when she pulled out of his embrace. Her own arms felt as if she'd ripped them from her body.

"Is that what you really want? I mean really?"

"Yes."

"How can you be so sure? So much has changed for us in these last few days."

He inhaled and pushed his fingers through his hair. "I know it sounds crazy. Two or three months ago I'd have laughed in your face if you suggested my leaving the firm, wanting to have a family."

He reached out and placed both of his hands on her cheeks and kissed her softly on the lips. The room spun around them. "When I'm with you, I feel more like myself than I ever felt in Manhattan. Every friend I had there held a knife to my back, waiting for me to make one mistake so they could move in for the kill. I don't have to watch my back when I'm with you. I don't want to play that game anymore. I want what's good and real. I want you, Cara."

The knot in her chest slipped free. She trembled beneath his touch. "The way you say it, it all makes sense."

A tide of emotion rolled over her. Devin pulled her into his arms and covered her mouth with his. She devoured his kiss, grazing her tongue against his lip until he opened up to her. If she'd ever wanted to fight this passion that had been building in them, she suddenly couldn't remember why. In her mind, all she could think of was how every moment before was meant to lead up to this one moment when she and Devin would finally give their love to each other fully.

Her hands had a mind of their own. She pulled and yanked at his shirt, until she was free to bury her fingers in the dark matte of his chest hair. His muscles grew taut beneath her touch and she reveled in his response, wanting more of it.

She'd dreamed of being in Devin's arms, of how hot and strong he'd feel, making love until he'd possessed every ounce of her soul. And there she was, with Devin, plunging into the fire he'd ignited, burning with each stroke of his hands.

He stepped back and dropped to the bed, bringing her with him. Cara straddled him, kissing, tasting him as if she couldn't get enough. With one quick motion, she pulled her T-shirt over her head. Her bra followed just as quickly, and then her upper body was bare. As much as she longed to reach forward and feel Devin's burning skin against her breasts, she forced herself to hold back, allowing him to take pleasure in seeing her.

His chest heaved as his eyes raked over breasts, inflaming her senses. Lord, she would never forget the hunger in his eyes, or the pure love she found there.

"I want you, too, Devin," she whispered, choking back a sob filled with emotion. "I want to make lo-"

He rolled over her, kissing her like a starved man who'd finally found repast, searching, withdrawing over and over until a soft moan crept up her throat. He kissed her there, where the sweet sounds of her desire cried out. He made a trail of moist kisses down her neck, her shoulders, until he reached her heaving breast. He lingered there, taking pleasure with his mouth, driving her insane in the process.

The barrier made by the remainder of their clothes did nothing to hide his hard arousal pressing against her thigh. She swore she heard him curse as he pulled his mouth away and began grappling with the belt on his denim shorts. She took that moment to free herself of the rest of her clothes, kicking them to the floor.

And then they were both gloriously naked, stripped of clothes and naked with raw emotion. With each lingering gaze, and cry of building passion, their feelings were crystal clear. It was as if a sheet had been pulled over their heads for seventeen years and only now, as they found fulfillment in each others arms, was it lifted.

Devin ran his hand down the outside of her leg and worked his way back up the inside of her thigh. His fingers gently worked the soft moist spot at the apex of her legs with delightful expertise. Tossing her head back, she lifted her hips higher into his hand until his urgent massage made her cry out in delight.

She opened up to him, unable to bear the aching need building inside her. Wrapping her legs around him, she stroked him with the same urgency he'd created in her until his breathing became rough. Still, he held himself back from entering her, as if to leave no doubt in her mind he cherished every inch of her being. And so, the give and take of pleasure ensued in an erotic dance of touching, stroking, tasting of flesh, until both were on the brink of losing control.

He entered her, slowly first, as if hanging on to the tiniest thread of control. As she gazed into Devin's dark eyes, a hint of a smile played on his lips. She was his and he loved that fact. Trembling in his arms, she gave herself up to him and he drove himself inside her as deep as her body would allow. His chest heaved with every thrust and stroke. Digging her fingers into his hard shoulders, she held on and they rode the flame of passion bringing them higher and higher.

She was vaguely aware of him calling out her name and then again, as her whole body tightened, building higher and higher until she cascaded to the other side.

It took many minutes before she could breathe again. Rolling to her side, Devin gathered her up and curled her into his warm embrace until they drifted off to sleep.

Cara couldn't remember a morning she'd felt happier. She stretched her back and felt the tenderness making love with Devin had left in its wake. Smiling with contentment, she grazed Devin's cheek with her fingers as he lay beside her, and nuzzled her chest against his wide back.

How could she have thought making love with Devin would destroy them? It had been wonderful, more incredible than she thought possible. She lay next to him, breathing in the seductive scent of his skin mixed with the scent of lovemaking from the warm sheets. She couldn't fall back to sleep, but Devin looked much too peaceful to wake.

She grinned with delight the instant the idea popped into her head. She'd bring him breakfast in bed. Since she wasn't the usual rise and shine person, it would make it a nice surprise when he woke up to have breakfast and a hot pot of coffee waiting. She carefully eased herself off the bed so as not to disturb his slumber and pulled the guest menu from the night stand.

It was still early, but surely there'd be someone awake downstairs preparing for the morning breakfast in the dining room. All she needed to do was request it be sent to their room instead. If she called from the room first, she'd run the risk of spoiling the surprise if Devin overheard. Better to go downstairs and talk to the Innkeeper directly. That way she could carry the tray up to the room herself and rouse Devin in her own way when she returned.

Gathering her clothes from the floor, she tip-toed to the bathroom to freshen up, wishing she'd had a fresh pair of panties and a toothbrush. Perhaps the innkeeper, Mrs. Patterson had some toothpaste and toothbrushes she could purchase. While she was at it, she'd buy a fresh T-shirt for Devin, since the one he'd worn yesterday was bloodied.

A few minutes later, Cara skipped down the paneled staircase and rounded the corner from the main foyer, following the aroma of freshly ground coffee. Intuition and her nose told her where she'd find the kitchen. As usual, her nose was right on target as she pushed through the swinging kitchen door.

Mrs. Patterson looked up from the bread she'd been kneading and greeted Cara with a smile. "My you're up early after getting in so late."

Cara chuckled. "There's a first for everything." She went about requesting a breakfast tray she could bring up to her room. Mrs. Patterson quickly obliged by wrapping freshly baked corn muffins and maple bread, still warm from the oven, and placing them in a bread basket with sweet butter and homemade jam.

"It's a shame you had my husband return your bicycles to the shop last night," Mrs. Patterson said, handing her two linen napkins and a carafe of freshly brewed coffee. "The rain really cooled the air and the morning has already started out to be quite a beauty."

"We're leaving after breakfast."

Mrs. Patterson's face drew into a frown. "That's odd. I'm usually so good about remembering which guests are which. I was sure your room was booked for three nights."

"Perhaps the people who canceled before us."

Mrs. Patterson shook her head. "No, Mr. Michaels got the last cancellation. We haven't had any more since he booked the room last week. We had to turn away another couple last night because we were waiting on your reservation."

A flurry of emotions clouded Cara's thinking. *Last week?* "You must be mistaken. We hadn't planned on staying in Nantucket."

Mrs. Patterson's face registered as much confusion as Cara felt. "If you'd like, I'll check the registration."

A warning voice whispered in her ear. "Please, do," Cara answered, not sure if she really wanted to know.

Chapter Twelve

Devin noticed the stiffness in Cara as soon as she'd come back to the room with breakfast. What seemed like a romantic gesture on her part only puzzled him in the end. He'd suggested they stay and take advantage of the room for the next few days, but she coolly insisted on leaving Nantucket as soon as they were through with breakfast.

Silence hung between them like a curtain keeping out the sunshine all the way to Steamboat Wharf where they boarded the ferry. Through the cries of the seagulls, the chatter of people boarding the boats, to the crash of boxes being unloaded from a freight, the silence was deafening. He didn't know how much more he could take. What had happened that wound Cara up into this tight knot? Was she already regretting their love making?

Devin vaguely recalled one of the tourists saying that it was tradition to throw two pennies into the water as the ferry sailed by Brant Point. It meant that you'd be coming back to Nantucket. Digging deep into the pocket of his shorts, he pulled out a few coins. "Here, toss these in."

"What's this for?" Her glance was slightly chilling.

"It's tradition. It means that we'll return to Nantucket someday."

Cara took the pennies from Devin, but instead of throwing them into the water, she clenched them in her fist.

"Maybe we can come back on our honeymoon," he said, resting his arm on her shoulder.

She straightened her back and faced him, her lips tight as if she were trying to hold on to control. "Tell me. How were you able to get a room at one of the best Bed and Breakfasts on Nantucket at the last minute?"

He shrugged. "Luck. Someone canceled."

"When?" She lifted her chin just slightly. Her voice was accusing, and he knew instantly that he'd been caught.

"I have no idea when they-"

"No, I mean you. When did *you* book the room?"

He'd called around to several inns on the island the night after Ruthie suggested he bring Cara to Nantucket. With every call, he was told the island was booked solid. He'd made an offer to give a hefty bonus to the person who could find him a room at any inn on such short notice. He wasn't disappointed when less than fifteen minutes later he got a call from Graystone informing him they'd just had a cancellation. He grabbed the room on the chance he and Cara decided to come to the island. He should have known Cara would become suspicious.

Yes, it had been premeditated. Guilty as caught.

"I booked a room a few days ago."

She closed her eyes and exhaled slowly, as if trying to remain calm. "Five days ago, to be exact. I only mentioned coming to Nantucket the other day. Why didn't you tell me then that you'd already booked a room— *one room*—here for us?"

"It's not what you're thinking."

"Oh, no? And just what am I thinking?" She scoped the immediate area before proceeding in a lower voice. "We made love last night, Devin. I thought something special had happened for us."

"It did."

"And now I find that you had the whole thing planned all along!"

"You're the one that asked me—"

"Save it, Devin. My mother put you up to this, didn't she?"

She didn't want to hear what he had to say. He could see by her set jaw and the way she folded her arms across her chest she'd already made up her mind that she'd been duped.

What was killing him the most was that she hated him for it.

"Believe me, I was going to tell you about the room when we got back to town. I was hoping we'd have a chance to talk, and I could convince you to stay. But then I hit that damned rock and fell and..."

Her eyebrows stretched on her forehead. "Was that planned, too?"

"Of course not!" Although, it served him right for paying more attention to the way Cara's hips rocked back and forth as she pedaled, than where he was going. If he had, he wouldn't have this incredible egg on his forehead. But then maybe last night would never have happened, either.

"Okay, so maybe I'm guilty of keeping secret the fact that I booked a room for us. That doesn't change how we feel about each other. It doesn't change last night."

He touched her arm and felt her tension ease slightly. "There's so much more I wanted to tell you last night. But I couldn't. Every time I looked at you I just wanted to hold you in my arms. And once you were there all I could thinking of was how much I wanted to make love to you. All the talk of the plans—"

Cara snapped her gaze at him in disbelief. "You mean, there's more?"

Devin took a deep breath and steeled himself. *Here we go.* "The wedding on Labor day."

Her expression was blank. "My parents' wedding."

He hesitated. "Our wedding."

Cara's mouth flew open, but no sound came out. "You've got to be kidding me."

He shook his head.

Her eyes were cold and accusing. "You've been in cahoots with my mother all along?"

"You're wrong."

"Stay away from me, Devin."

Spinning on her heels, she stomped off through the crowd of people, almost crashing into a group holding their bikes.

"Where are you going?" he called after her.

She didn't answer. And he didn't follow. She was spitting angry and he knew she needed space before he could even attempt to get her to see the truth. And he was going to give her that space. No matter how much it killed him. Besides, it wasn't as if she could run very far. They were on a damned ferry boat.

Cara kept moving around the ferry until she found a secluded place in the bowels of the ferry, just outside the engine room. The hum of the engine drowned out her soft sobs as she slumped on a red cushioned chair.

How could Devin do this to her? She expected this sort of behavior from her mother. She'd lived her whole life fighting it. But Devin?

When they'd made love, she thought she had forever in her arms. With every kiss and caress from Devin she'd envisioned their life together, loving each other, all the beautiful babies they'd make. It had seemed so perfect.

Too perfect, she now realized.

Last night she thought her dreams had been coming true. But it had all been a lie. After learning how Devin planned this whole trip and kept it secret, how could she believe that all those promises he'd made last night weren't lies too?

She drew in a deep breath of air and almost choked, a little from her sobs and from the diesel exhaust seeping out of the engine room.

When Devin finally found her a good hour later, she'd managed to compose herself enough to talk coherently.

His face was drawn when he appeared at the bottom of the metal staircase, as if he'd spent the last hour waiting for his turn in the noose. With her own emotions at battle, she wasn't sure if she wanted to run into his arms or hand him the rope.

"I don't understand, Devin. Why didn't you tell me?"

"I wanted to. Every time you looked at me, I knew how you felt. But you kept pulling away and I just couldn't figure out what was holding us back. Then when Roger left..."

He slumped down on the chair next to her. His thigh grazed the bare skin of her thigh sending a warm trail through the rest of her body. Everything about Devin was warm and comforting.

"Do you love him?"

"That's not what this is about, Devin."

"Are you sure?" he persisted. "You're angry with me for keeping secrets. My reasons are pretty self explanatory. I love you and I'm trying my damnedest to win your love. But every time I ask you this simple question, you can't seem to give me a straight answer."

He swallowed hard, his jaw tight with tension.

She didn't answer. What could she say after all that had transpired last night? The answer was glaring, but she knew he needed to hear it.

"I have a lot of time invested in Roger."

Devin made a face and glared at her for a lingering moment. "Will you listen to yourself? You talk about him like he's a stock option. Like he's some damned mutual fund you're going to get a penalty on for early withdrawal. That's so clinical."

"That's my relationship with Roger in a nutshell," she muttered.

"Do you love me?"

Her head was swimming and her heart pounded in her chest as if it were about to explode. *Coward,* she screamed silently.

When she didn't answer, he went one step further. "Is that why you're pulling away from us? Because you're afraid of loving me?"

"Don't go there, Devin. Not now."

One look on his face and she knew he understood her much more than she did herself.

"You do love me, and it scares the hell out of you, doesn't it? You can't be safe with me. You have to be vulnerable. That's the part of this you can't stand. You love that what we have is special and real, but it means you have to give up control if you give up your heart."

She had to get away from him before she said something she'd regret. Before the last threads of their relationship was destroyed.

But mostly, she realized, she needed to get away because she knew without any reservation that he was one hundred percent correct. Everything about loving Devin scared her to death. Things were changing between them already. It was all too much. She wanted the old Devin back. The one who didn't keep secrets from her. The friend who didn't side with her mother to make her into someone she couldn't be.

She stood up and wiped her palms on her shorts. "My whole life my mother has pushed me to have the kind of life she wanted for me, totally discounting what I want. She's always wanted me to marry you."

He curled his fingers around her upper arm before she could bolt and swung her around to look at him. "And you're so hell-bent on proving her wrong that you're willing to risk losing us in the process."

"Dammit, Devin, you're supposed to me on my side. I'm trying to keep us from losing our friendship again. Last night wasn't us. It was calculated."

He laughed sardonically. "It was more of you and me than we ever cared to admit before."

She wrenched her arm free and bolted toward the stairs. Holding both sides of the rail, she took the steps two at a time with Devin on her heels.

"You're scared and you're running away from us." he called from behind.

"There isn't any *us*."

She heard his cynical laugh behind her. "That's right, you have your career. You don't need anything or anyone else."

Her anger doubled and tripled before she was able to gain enough control to breathe again. She swung around to face him at the top of the stairs.

"And you've been conspiring with my mother all along with this secret wedding."

"I only found out about the wedding the other day. That was after I knew how I felt about you. Before that I still believed the wedding was for your parents."

He reached out and touched her, which did wonders to assuage her anger, but only to build on the primal need they'd succumbed to last night.

She blinked hard. "Devin, we should have never gone as far as we did. Can't you see what this is doing? What my mother's manipulation has done to us?"

His voice was low as he responded. "Your mother had nothing to do with the way you responded to me last night."

Her cheeks flamed and she felt her body grow warm remembering Devin's strong hands touching her breast, stroking the inside of her thighs. She closed her eyes and whispered, "No, but I don't want to lose you."

"So much so that you'd rather play it safe with a man you don't love? You don't love Roger. Don't bother trying to deny it because I won't believe it if you tell me you love him now."

She didn't try. Devin had been right. Roger had been her safety net. The boat would never be rocked and her world would always remain intact, under her control, if she stayed with him. There'd be no changes, no surprises. The fact that her mother couldn't stand him was just an added bonus in a game she and her mother had always played. That realization left a bitter taste in her mouth.

Too much of her world was coming apart at the seams. All her dreams and goals had taken on a new dimension. The very foundation of her life was shifting.

Devin touched her face and brushed his thumb along her cheek. The deep timbre of his voice made everything he said seem so simple. "Life's not that cut and dry, Cara. You don't take each step knowing where you'll end up in advance. Sometimes life is just a crap shoot. Sometimes you have to risk losing everything to get what it is you really want."

She gently pulled his hand away. "I'm not a gambler, Devin. I need something I can count on. I always thought I could count on you."

"You still can."

"I don't want to lose that."

The horn sounded and a flurry of people started advancing toward the exit. Cara sprinted until she fell into step with them. She knew Devin would be right behind her, but she couldn't stay on the boat and cry in front of everyone. She needed Devin, but not here and not like this.

As soon as the ferry docked, she ran down the ramp, vaguely aware of how rudely she was pushing herself past the other people in line. When she reached the dock, she waited for Devin to catch up.

In his expression, she saw the hurt and fear of a dejected man. She didn't want to see Devin as the man she was desperately in love with. She wanted him to be her friend. She wanted it to be the way it was, securely tucked away in a safe harbor called the past.

"I need my best friend, too, Cara. For the rest of my life, everyday in my bed and in my heart." He pressed his fist against his chest and squeezed his hand. "For always. That's why we can't let this go."

She didn't hide the willful tear that rolled down her cheek. Devin was right. She had been holding her own secrets tight to her chest.

"Roger asked me to marry him."

The blood drained from his face right before her very eyes. He took one big step backward as if she'd just slapped him across the face. "What did you say?" he rasped, his jaw tight.

"He asked me to—"

"Dammit, I heard that part. What was your answer?"

"That I needed some space."

He swallowed hard. His voice was weak when he spoke. "Why didn't you tell me all this yesterday, *last night*?"

"I just wanted to be with you. I didn't want to think about anything else."

He shook his head as if in disbelief. "You can't have it both ways, Cara. I won't share your love with him."

"I'm not asking you to share," she insisted.

"What do you call it then? We've already taken our relationship too far. There's no going back now."

A hot tear trickled down her cheek. "I needed my best friend, Devin. I needed you."

He took her hands and brought them to his lips, kissing them softly. Desire swirled through her body with the memory of just how those kisses effected her and she pulled her hands away.

"Well here I am in the flesh. The man you choose to marry should be your best friend. And that's me, Cara. Why can't you see that?"

"It's not that simple."

"For me, it is. In my life, it's all or nothing. If you choose to be with him, then we lose. I won't stand by watching you love another man. I won't."

The mid-morning sun beat down on her as if it were pounding her to the ground. Maybe because she felt like she just been beaten herself. By circumstance and by fear.

She could only watch as Devin charged through the crowd walking along the wharf. Inside she was raw like an open gash.

Devin was right. And she was being a coward. At that moment, feeling as low as she was, all she wanted was Devin's arms to comfort her when she should have wanted Roger.

The man you choose to marry should be your best friend. Devin *was* her best friend. And she'd just done her damnedest to drive him away.

Chapter Thirteen

"Are you sure you won't stay until after Labor Day?" Ruthie said, sitting on the bed next to Cara's half filled suitcase. Her mother did nothing to hide her disappointment that Cara had decided to return to Boston earlier than she'd originally planned.

Cara dropped her cosmetic case into her suitcase. Much as she hated all the lies and manipulation, Cara had always found it difficult to stay angry with her mother. No matter what, she loved her unconditionally.

"Louise has been having false labor. Her baby is going to be here any day now and I need to get back to work to get a clear head about what is going on before she leaves."

"You need to be back here for the wedding."

What she needed was to get back to Boston and plant herself firmly in her old life. She hadn't talked to Devin since their argument and he'd run off. For all she knew, he probably thought she'd gone back to Boston to marry Roger.

Of course, nothing could have been further from the truth. No matter what happened from this point on in her relationship with Devin, she knew she couldn't stay with Roger. She wasn't in love with him. Plain and simple. And it had taken all the heartache and crying she'd done over Devin to come to that realization.

She'd come back here, locked herself in her room, half hoping Devin would come after her, half knowing he wouldn't. Now she didn't know how she was going to undo the mess she'd made.

One thing she did know for sure, this charade she'd been playing with her mother had gone too far.

"Mom, I know the wedding isn't for you and Daddy."

To her credit, Ruthie gave up the charade as well. "Devin told you?"

Cara nodded, all the anger she'd had pent up over her mother's deception was long gone. "I know your intentions were good. But I can't marry Devin just because you want me to give you grandchildren."

Ruthie sighed heavily. "The only thing I really want is for my daughter to be happy. And judging by the way you've been moping around for the last few days, you're far from it."

Cara closed her eyes, trying her best to keep the tears that threatened her from falling. Lord knows she'd shed enough trying to figure out why she was being so stubborn. Even after all the heartache and tears, she still couldn't bring herself to gamble her friendship with Devin away. They'd been there and done that seventeen years ago. And they'd lost. She didn't want to lose again.

She drew in a steadying breath. Time and distance is what she needed to put things back into perspective. She needed to plant herself firmly in her old routine and decide which direction to turn.

Except clarity was the last thing she got when she returned to her Back Bay condo later that afternoon. Every time the phone rang, she ran to answer it, expecting it to be Devin. But it never was. It left her lots of idle time to sift through paperwork and check on orders she'd already checked and to think...

How could her mother have actually thought she'd go through with an arranged marriage? It was completely archaic and, well, stupid. She was not the marrying kind of woman. She'd said that all along and that was all there was to it.

Her stomach ached from the greasy potato chips she'd eaten for break-fast and she clutched her stomach to ease the pain.

Devin. As angry as she was with him for playing along with her moth-er's game, damn, she loved him. Could it really be like he said? Could they really have it all and a family, too?

We'd make an awesome team. She'd replayed the words over and over again until her head hurt. She rubbed the soft aching spot at her temple and slouched back on her sofa. She and Devin, they *would* make an in-credible team.

Sometimes life is just a crap shoot. Sometimes you have to risk losing everything to get what it is you really want.

Distance had not given her the answers she wanted. It had only forced her to look at the questions she'd been running away from. She needed to talk to Devin. Only then would the answers come clearly.

But first, she needed to straighten out things with Roger. What she needed to say wasn't going to be easy, and she wasn't sure how either one of them would handle it, but she had a two-carat reason for trying. With her decision made, her stomach suddenly felt a little better and her head a little lighter.

She didn't bother to reach Roger until well into the evening. That's the way things had always been. Except before, she'd always been work-ing, too. She'd had the whole afternoon to sit and think about exactly what she was going to say. She'd sat in her studio, staring at the bolts of fabric and odds and ends, rehearsing out loud her speech about why things just weren't going to work between them.

Standing outside his apartment later that evening, she felt confident, and almost herself again. Until the door swung open and she saw Roger's face.

"We need to talk," she said.

In the end, Roger's reaction to their breakup was surprisingly good. He'd admitted the changes in her mood had frightened him, but he thought that marriage was all it would take to change things back to the smooth existence they'd always had. He was adamant that children were not part of his future. When she left an hour later, he gave her a long hug at the door and she was glad that it was over.

If only she'd taken Devin's advice earlier and talked to Roger about her feelings, things wouldn't have gotten so fouled up.

She'd chosen to follow her heart and talk to her best friend instead.

Devin yanked at the collar of his stiffly starched tuxedo shirt and fiddled with the black tie choking him. He couldn't believe he let Ruthie convince him this little plan to go through with the wedding was going to work.

He hadn't seen or heard from Cara since that day on the ferry. At first he thought she'd need some time and he was going to give it to her for however long it took for her to see that they belonged together.

He'd wrapped himself around the Palmer case, putting together the necessary paperwork for appeal so he could prove the so called evidence the state had against Wendell Palmer was bogus. After much haggling, the judge had agreed to an appeal. The cloud of doubt hanging over him about his career seemed a little clearer and he actually felt good about what he did for a living for the first time in a long time.

Now if he could only get Cara to see things a little more clearly. He had to be the biggest fool to think Cara would actually show up here today and marry him today after the way she'd raced off. So what was he doing dressed in a tuxedo on the hottest Labor Day in history, waiting for a bride that was never going to show?

Yeah, he was a fool all right. And he was in love. That pretty much summed it up.

"She's not coming," he ground out nervously, pacing back and forth like an expecting father.

Ruthie stilled him and fiddled with his tie, her usual jovial smile planted on her face. She was dressed in a cream colored chiffon dress. Her hair looked stiff from too much hairspray meant to combat the humidity.

Her voice was confident when she spoke. "Don't you worry. You don't know my Cara the way I do."

"She's too damn stubborn," Devin sputtered, darting a glance to the double doors at the back of the church, willing Cara to appear there.

"Hmmm. You're right about that."

"She's headstrong."

"Right again."

"She can be impossibly irrational."

Ruthie chuckled and patted his shoulder. "And she's completely in love with you. She's always been."

Devin's breath caught in his throat. Was she? After that glorious night they'd made love in Nantucket, he would have bet his last nickel Cara loved him as deeply as he loved her. But she'd never uttered the words.

"Don't worry yourself so much," Ruthie said. "You'll sweat in your tux and you look much too handsome for that. I know my Cara. She'll be here."

Cara's heart fell through the sand when she saw the "For Rent" sign hanging in the window of Devin's cottage. Except, it wasn't really Devin's cottage. He'd only rented it to come here for her birthday and decide what he wanted to do with his life. Apparently he'd made his decision and she wasn't part of it.

The headlines in the *Boston Globe* that morning buzzed about how Devin Michaels had scored another legal victory. The appeals judge had decided to listen to Devin's case. Cara had no doubt he'd score yet another legal victory. With so much work to do on the case, he'd probably gone back to Manhattan.

How could she have been so stupid? Cara chided herself as she ran down the beach toward her parents' home. Maybe they hadn't left yet. Maybe the movers were still putting the furniture on the truck and she still had time to find out where Devin had gone.

As she approached the house, she paused and leaned over, resting her hands on her knees, trying to catch her breath. The movers were there. But instead of loading furniture on, the were unloading. The new owners were nowhere in sight. But neither was her family. They had already left town without her having a chance to say good-bye.

Cara did nothing to hold back the tears rolling down her burning cheeks.

She'd been so pigheaded, trying to prove everyone wrong she couldn't see that she was the one who'd been wrong.

So wrong.

She loved Devin. She always had and always would. But she'd gone ahead and pushed him away one too many times.

She forced air into her lungs to help stop her sobbing. As she walked through the white picket gate, sidestepping the strange men unloading boxes and chairs, she felt lonely. The only signs that she and her family had called this house home were the names etched in the cement walkway leading up to the front porch. She and Manny had "helped" their father build the walk when they were kids. They'd put their hand print in the cement before it dried. Her mother scribbled the names.

She sat cross-legged on the walk, feeling the gritty sand embedded there dig into her thighs. With her hand splayed, she touched the tiny print she'd made years ago. Back then her only ambition was to please her parents. How had she gotten so headstrong and stubborn that she'd sabotage her own happiness with Devin just to prove them wrong?

A crunching sound on the pavement caused her to look up. She was met by her brother Manny's warm smile.

"That was a long time ago, wasn't it?" Manny held his arms open wide and Cara rushed up to give her brother a hug. "I knew I'd find you here. Everyone's been worried."

"I know. I should have been here to see Mom and Dad off," she sobbed. "I've been so stupid."

"So I've heard."

She pulled away, wiping her tears from her cheeks as she looked at him. It amazed her that after all this time seeing him in the collar, she still could look at Manny and see the snotty little brother he'd always been to her. "Who's been talking about me?"

He laughed. "Everyone! When the bride doesn't show up for her own wedding, people start to talk."

"What do—you mean they're all down at the church...waiting for me?"

"Yes. Mom sent me back here to see if I could find you. Devin's having a coronary."

Her eyes flew open wide. "Devin's there!?"

Manny chuckled. "It's usually customary for the groom to be present at the wedding, too."

"Wedding," she muttered. Yes, it was Labor Day. It was supposed to be the day her parents would renew their wedding vows. Or rather, she and Devin would become man and wife.

"I thought he'd gone back to Manhattan."

Manny shook his head. "You can't get rid of Devin that easy. Not this time anyway." He pointed to the moving van. "This is all his stuff."

Tears rolled down Cara's cheeks and she trembled. "Devin bought the house?" She couldn't believe it. This must have been one of the "plans" Devin had mentioned while they were in Nantucket. Except she'd been too stubborn to listen to him.

Manny bent down and kissed her cheek. "Come on, Sis. This isn't just Mom's day, it belongs to you and Devin, too. Your gown is down at the church. All we have to do is get you there."

The organist started to play the traditional wedding march as Harold took Cara by the arm. She was wearing the dress intended to be a brides-maid's dress for her mother and father's ceremony. But then, of course, her mother had planned this whole affair all along with Cara being the center of attention. It was *her* wedding day.

"Wait, Daddy."

Harold groaned and checked the watch on his wrist. "What now?"

"I need to see Devin."

He grinned. "Honey, you have the rest of your life."

"No, I need to see him before we get married."

"Why?"

"I just do."

"Are you sure?"

Cara nodded. "Please?"

Harold heaved a sigh. "Okay, but you're mother won't be too happy about the groom seeing you in your dress before the wedding."

Cocking her head, she sputtered, "All of the sudden she's going to pull tradition on me?"

He nodded. "You have a point, dear. I'll see if I can smuggle him back here without your mother catching wind of it."

She threw her arms around her father. "Thank you, Daddy."

As the door closed, Cara closed her eyes and took a deep breath. She'd never told Devin she loved him. Somehow, that was vitally important for her to do *before* they became man and wife. Nothing else mattered more than that. The cake could melt in the heat, the balloons could pop, the canopy on the back lawn of the rectory could collapse, and all the flowers in Westport could go ahead and wilt in the sun.

But it was important that Devin knew she was marrying him because she loved him more than anything else in the world. She always had and she always would. She needed to say it and he deserved to hear it from her first, before she professed it in front of a church filled with people.

Cara paced the room, smoothing down the skirt of her dress with her sweaty palms. She turned to the sound of the knock on the door and waited for it to open before she was able to breathe again.

Devin's worried face greeted her. He looked bewildered, tired, and absolutely the most wonderful sight a girl could ever hope for. His black tuxedo was neat as a pin and he filled out every inch of it as if it were tailor-formed to his body.

It took visible effort for him to breathe, too, she noticed as he carefully closed the door to the bride's room behind him and took a few steps into the room. His face was like that of a starving man who'd finally had a banquet laid out in front of him.

"You look beautiful," he whispered, then took in a deep breath, stretching the fabric of his tuxedo jacket against his chest.

She couldn't help but feel giddy and lightheaded. "Do you really think so?"

He smiled at her shocked expression. "I always have."

She looked down at the bouquet of tiny pink and white princess roses in her hand. "What are we doing here?"

"I thought we were getting married." For a fleeting second a worried expression clouded his smile. "Are we?"

"I'm here, aren't I?" No, that wasn't it. That's not what she wanted to say. "You were right. I was scared, Devin. The way I behaved, it was never that I didn't want to be with you. So much was changing around me, Mom and Dad moving to Florida, me re-evaluating my life, you coming back to Westport. I was scared of all that change and I thought, if I could just keep us the way we were, you wouldn't leave, too."

She bit her bottom lip to keep it from quivering.

"I just want you to be the first to hear me say how much I truly love you."

He breathed a sigh of relief and advanced toward her. She wanted so much for him to take her in his arms and melt the uncertainty away, but there was still so much that needed to be said. She held up her hand to keep him from his quest and his expression collapsed.

"Is that really enough, Dev? We've been down this road before. I don't want to blow it."

"That's not going to happen," he assured her with a smile. "Seventeen years ago we weren't ready to love each other. Our ambition never would have survived if our love did. One of us would have had to give up our dreams for the other to realize theirs. I had to leave you then because I couldn't face us having to choose. But we don't have to make that choice anymore."

"Are you sure? This is all so crazy."

"Sure it is. But what's even crazier is if we let this chance slip away from us." He looked at her, pleading like a desperate man about to hang on the noose. "I love you, Cara. Nothing else matters as much as that anymore. Nothing."

It was if the clouds parted and the heavens were shining down on them. It all made sense with Devin, just like she knew it would. Time had seasoned them enough to realize what was important.

She hooked her arm around his and reached up, giving him a sound kiss on the mouth. "I guess we've waited long enough, huh?"

He smiled his answer and led her to the door. After opening it a crack, she pushed back the door and swung around, a sinking feeling flooding her stomach.

"The marriage license," she gasped, putting her hand over her mouth.

"What about it?"

"My mother must have had it forged. It's not legal!"

Devin returned a devilish grin, pulling her into his arms. "I won't tell if you won't."

She pushed at his chest, not finding the same humor he found in their predicament. "I finally have all that I want right here in my arms and I'll be damned if I'm going to let it go now on a minor technicality. I want **this** marriage contract to be legal!"

"Don't worry," he whispered, opening the door. "Manny is used to your mother's antics, remember? He's got another marriage license for us to sign right after the ceremony. This marriage contract is legal."

Minutes later, with her arm hooked on her father's, staring at Devin through the sheer fabric of her veil, she realized, in their hearts, it had always been.

If you enjoyed this novel, why not try Lisa Mondello's first novel, *Nothing But Trouble*? It is also available from Domhan Books in paperback and e formats.

1-58345-323-7 Millennium
1-58345-324-5 Rocket
1-58345-349-0 paper
1-58345-325-3 e book

Melanie Summers, a feisty zoologist with big dreams, must spend a month in the Wyoming wilderness in order to satisfy a deal made with her father. Stoney Buxton is a hard-driving cowboy with simple values who needs to raise quick money to save the family ranch. Re-entering the rodeo circuit seems like the best way to get the money he needs until Melanie Summers shows up at his ranch flashing easy money. To everyone else, her offer seems like the answer to all his prayers. But one look at her long legs and pouting lips and Stoney know this high society gal is going to be nothing but trouble for his cowboy heart.

She cocked her head. "Don't be foolish. This could help both of us. You don't look like the type of man to shy away from honest money."
He drew in a deep breath and could hardly look her in the eye.
"I'm not looking for you to carry my bags or draw the bath water," she said when he didn't respond.
His laugh was rich and hard. He dipped his gaze beneath his dusty leather hat, shaking his head. When he lifted his head again, she saw them. He had dimples. Deep, and completely adorable. Her heart betrayed her confidence and fluttered wildly.
"Good, because you'd be sadly disappointed."
She forced air into her lungs and placed her hand on her chest to steady her rampant heartbeat.
He took a long appraising look at her, much like a man does when he finds a woman attractive, as if he was weighing the option to pass her by or dip his head and kiss her waiting lips. It filled her with a strange sense of longing she couldn't define.
"I may be stubborn, lady, but I'm far from dumb."
Her eyes widened. She was almost afraid to believe her good fortune. "So what are you saying? You'll help me?"